LIVESTOCK
Horror Stories From the Un-Herd

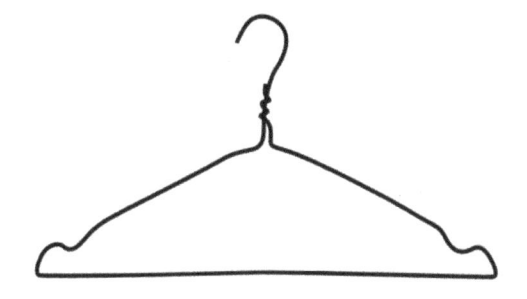

Collected by: Voices From the Mausoleum
Edited by: Tasha Reynolds
Cover Art by: Ruth Anna Evans

Table of Contents

Foreword- Tasha Reynolds.................... 5

A Good Day- Ruth Anna Evans............................ 9

A Paring Down- Sarah Dropek 22

Urban Forestry- Maureen O' Leary.................. 39

The Quantum Mixtapes of New Venus- Joan Wendland............................ 48

Cuckoo- Kay Hanifen........................... 58

Lex Talionis- M. Edusa........................ 73

The Old Ways-Christiane Erwin 94

Help is on the Way- Cat Voleur...................... 108

Bedrest- Yvonne Dutchover........................... 115

The Three Undoings of Della Rae- Sabrina Voerman 159

Mercy- Kyra R. Tores...................................... 174

And They Shall Be Changed- Hazel Ragaire ... 182

Go Down Swinging- Tiffany Michelle Brown . 190

Witch's Heart- Stephanie Parent 199

Half-Mile- H. Everend 220

The Heartbeat- Melinda N. Brunson 227

The Burden- Angel Krause 240

Dedication

This is a collection of stories for women. A reminder we see and hear you. This is for anyone raised to believe they owed the world something. This is for men who stand by our sides, and a reminder to those who do not. This is for you. All of you. All of us.

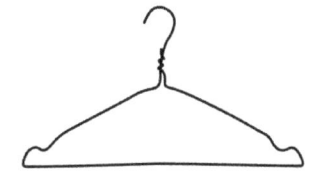

Foreword- Tasha Reynolds

I'd never run through so many different emotions in such a short period of time. At first, there was disbelief. It's 2022… there's no way we'd really take that big of a step back… right?

Wrong.

Then there was the all-encompassing fire that coursed from my head to the tips of my toes – an absolute rage that something like this wasn't just possible, but reality. Some of the *women* I work with, said things I couldn't even wrap my head around. "This will just force women to be held accountable for their actions." "I don't know why women want to be equal to men anyways." "If they didn't want a child then they should have taken necessary steps to avoid it, or just said 'no'."

The despair was next, as I began to realize just how many people out there, men and women alike, didn't see anything wrong with what was happening.

Terror settled into my bones. My little sister is fifteen. Several of my friends have little girls, and I cringed thinking about what this could mean for their futures.

A charity anthology seemed like a great way to provide a variety of options for folks to contribute to a good cause (women's health/rights), and at the same time, offer women the opportunity to vent about the real horrors unfolding and what nightmares it brought to the forefront. Angel and I announced the call, listed guidelines, and provided our sites as additional sources of information. People shared it like crazy! The support was amazing and provided some much-needed hope.

We received the first story, and then a second. Except… the second email was from a man who admitted he knew we were only accepting submissions from women but insisted that he had a story *he* felt would be a good fit. I politely thanked him for his interest, reminded him that we were only accepting submissions from women, and he continued to try and hype himself (and his story) up. It took everything in me not to point out that he was exactly the type of man that created this whole situation in the first place – especially when I read the story and it was the most glaring example, I'd ever seen of someone trying to write from a perspective they clearly had no knowledge of.

He finally let it be, and Livestock ended up forming a fiery collection of stories from some amazing women. Every time I read them, my blood started boiling again over what has happened, and what could potentially happen. Voices from the Mausoleum made great choices in designing Livestock, invested a tremendous amount of her time and efforts breathing life into this project, and it absolutely paid off.

What continues to be a source of hope is the outpouring of support from the horror community. There are pictures and footage of protests in the news that show men and women, young and old, from all walks of life, out in the streets to make their points. Huge crowds of people who will never quit fighting, who won't make things easy for those with power trying to push us backwards, congregated in cities everywhere.

So rage, ladies. Scream about the nightmares we have – the ones we refuse to accept. Make it clear where we stand and stick together. There will be no giving up or quiet acceptance of a future like that, and I dare them to try and ignore the force that we are!

"The question isn't who's going to let me; it's who is going to stop me."

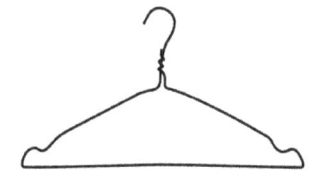

A Good Day- Ruth Anna Evans

Morgan gritted her teeth and turned up her music, trying to ignore the screaming of the baby. It put her nerves on edge. She tapped out a few more sentences, then wrinkled her nose.

Pulling her headphones off, she listened for a second. The baby was now gurgling and cooing in the other room.

"Tim, the litter box smells!" she shouted.

"Okay, babe, I'll get it in a minute."

"Thanks!" She typed a bit more of her story, distracted by the smell. It was really bad, like ammonia and Febreeze. "What are you doing in there?"

"Changing Timmy again. I just gave him a bath and he already had a blowout." Tim sounded tired. Morgan felt a shot of guilt, knowing she should hop up and scoop the litter box herself, but also knowing that he would do it if she waited.

She waited.

A few minutes later, her husband walked by carrying a grocery bag, headed for the back room. Thank goodness.

"How's the writing going?"

"Slowly but surely," she answered as she always did. He was curious about what she was writing, but she never offered to let him take a peek. When she was published, then he could read it.

"I think one of us needs to go to the Dollar Store," he said loudly from the back room. "We need more litter."

Was he hinting that she should go? Morgan tapped a little louder. "I'm kind of busy here, would you be able to do it?"

The truth was, she didn't want to do housework, errands, or childcare of any sort. All she wanted to do was write, sleep, and eat. It was all she'd ever wanted to do.

When Morgan had discovered she was pregnant, she had called for an appointment to get the abortion pill. Babies were loud and gross and needy. She never understood her friends' desperate desire to give up their personal freedom—and their bodies—for a small, shitty tyrant. But when they checked her at the clinic, she was seven weeks along. The abortion pill was only allowed up to five. They sent her home with some coupons for diapers and a handout about the criminal penalties if she sought an abortion elsewhere.

She had no choice.

So she got fat, popped the baby out, and went straight back to her novel-in-progress. She winced when she remembered how hard Tim had begged her to try breastfeeding. But attaching a sucking infant to her nipples was just too weird.

Tim washed his hands and got his wallet. "I'll be back in a minute," he said. He kissed her on top of her head and shut the door gently behind him. He always respected her writing time. It was one of the reasons she stayed married to him. That and the dishes.

Morgan got three pages done before little Timmy started squalling. *Tim will be home soon*, she told herself. She tried to block it out and keep typing, but then her phone was ringing.

"Goddammit!" She picked up her phone. It was an unknown number, but it was local. She swiped and answered, annoyed.

"Is this Morgan Simpson?"

"Yes?"

"This is Officer Nunley from the Henderson Police Department. Tim Simpson is your husband, correct?"

"Yes, why? What's going on? Is he ok?"

"I'm sorry to inform you of this, ma'am, but he's been involved in a car crash."

"Is he conscious? Why isn't he calling me?" Her stomach lurched.

"No ma'am. I'm afraid he's pretty badly injured, and he wasn't conscious when the ambulance left the scene to take him to Henderson Memorial."

Morgan moved to grab her keys and realized she was going to need to take Timmy with her. "Okay, I'm on my way. How bad is he?"

"We haven't received any updates from the hospital yet, but you'll want to hurry. Is there someone who can drive you, or are you okay to drive yourself?"

"Shit. Fuck. Okay. Okay, I'll be fine, I can drive myself. I'm on my way." She hung up and, pausing to save her work, went to grab the baby. The car seat was in Tim's car. The damn car seat was in Tim's car!

"What am I supposed to do with you?" Morgan held the baby out in front of her, grasping him under the armpits, his scrawny little legs dangling. He was still bawling, his bottom lip stuck out, his bald head flopped over, bright red.

She popped him under her arm and ran for the car, laying him down on the back seat and wrapping a seat belt around him a few times, then buckling it.

"It'll be fine," she mumbled at the baby. "You'll be fine. Just hush."

As she drove to the hospital, Timmy slid back and forth in the back of the car, tangled in the seat belt, squalling like a little pig. Morgan looked at him in her rearview mirror, hoping he didn't crack his head on something on top of everything else. That would have to be explained to people and she didn't have time.

She was more worried about her husband. He was unconscious after a car wreck. It could be really bad.

Don't die, Tim, please don't die, spun around and around her head. *I do not want to start changing diapers.*

She shook the thought away and pulled into the Emergency Room parking lot. She untangled Timmy from the seatbelt and carried him awkwardly inside. Usually his dad carried him. At the desk, she started to feel truly nervous. What was Tim going to look like? Was he going to be all twisted and bloody and gross?

"I'm so sorry about this," a kind brunette at the check-in said, full of sympathy. "I just need to see your ID and then I'll show you to his room."

Morgan realized she had left her purse in the car. She shuffled Timmy over to the nice lady and ran out to get it. When she returned, the baby had a hint of a smile on his face and was touching the woman's curly hair. The brunette looked at her a little sideways. Morgan knew it probably wasn't normal to just shove your baby at a stranger and run out of a building, but allowances had to be made. She was in what could be described as a tizzy.

Morgan handed over her ID, and the woman gave her Timmy back. He was such an awkward weight. She tried balancing him on her hip like she had seen other mothers do, but he just slid down. This was getting to be a lot.

"Um, you need to be supporting his head." The nurse said quietly.

Morgan sighed and shifted her arm so that the baby's head wasn't bobbing quite so wildly. They walked a short way down the antiseptic hallway and stopped in front of a room.

"You're going to need to prepare yourself," the nurse said gently. "The doctor will be in shortly. For now, just sit with him. Talk to him."

Morgan steeled herself and entered the room. Her husband had a tube shoved down his throat, and his chest was pumping up and down rhythmically. His neck was in a brace and his eyes were closed. The room smelled.

"Why does it smell like that in here?" Morgan asked the nurse. The nurse gave her a pitying look. "The CNA will be in soon to change him," she said, gesturing to a chair next to the bed.

Horrified but not knowing what else to do, Morgan sat. She moved the baby to her lap, where she tried to get him to sit up. He slumped and started crying.

Did you bring a bottle?

Morgan almost fell out of her chair. "Tim?"

He's hungry. Did you bring a bottle? The voice in her head was unmistakably Tim's. He sounded calm and kind but mildly concerned. His eyes were still closed, the ventilator making it impossible to speak even if he weren't unconscious.

Morgan poked Tim's hand. "Are you awake? Wake up!"

You're going to need to feed the baby, honey.

"I can't do this. You need to wake up."

Timmy was starting to wail louder.

Feed. The. Baby.

"Shit!" she said, turning the child and looking at him in the face. Why did babies always look like turnips when they were young? How were you supposed to love them when they were so ugly?

Morgan put the baby down in the chair and walked to the door, sticking her head out and calling, "Nurse?"

A new nurse, a petite woman with braids down her back, rounded the corner, looking willing to help but busy. She approached Morgan.

"The doctor will be here soon," she said. "What can I help you with?"

"You guys don't have any formula or anything do you? I think the baby is hungry."

The nurse—Reonna, according to her nametag—looked over Morgan's shoulder into the room where Timmy was screaming from the chair, his little hands in fists and his mouth open wide. The nurse pushed past Morgan and snatched up the baby.

"You can't leave him unattended in a chair like that! He could fall!"

What are you thinking, Morgan? I need you to get it together right now, Tim said in her head. *Be a mom, for God's sake!*

As a child, Morgan had never dreamed about being a mother. She had always half-hoped she was sterile. When she and Tim were dating and the issue had come up, she had hemmed and hawed her way through the conversations. He had ignored her reluctance, and when the birth control failed and the abortion plan failed and she had finally told him she was pregnant, he had been so excited. She had hoped that he would make up for her lack of enthusiasm.

But now he was stinking in a hospital bed, harassing her telepathically. This was not something she signed up for.

The nurse peeked in the back of Timmy's diaper.

"He needs changed," she said, warily handing him back to Morgan. "I'm going to find you a diaper and some formula." Her eyes softened. "I'm sure you left the house in a hurry. It's going to be okay."

Morgan didn't want to change the baby. She really didn't want to touch him, knowing that he was stewing in his own feces. She had done a few diapers when he was first born, and Tim had changed the rest when he saw how much she hated it.

Reonna left for the supplies and Morgan sat back down in the chair, holding Timmy away from her body and trying not to gag at the combined smells in the room.

You can do this, Tim's voice intruded on her thoughts again. He had regained his composure and she could hear that trying-to-be-patient tone he had with her sometimes. *He's your son.*

"He's your son more," she said out loud. "What am I supposed to do now?"

Tim's voice rose: *Try!*

A white-coated male doctor, young-looking and somewhat attractive except for a big mole on his chin, walked in the room. He had an iPad in his hands and kept his eyes on that while he talked to Morgan.

"Your husband's injuries are extensive," he said. "He has several broken bones, which we can fix, but our biggest concern is his brain. He hit his head very hard and there seems to be substantial damage."

"What are you going to do?"

"We'll monitor the swelling. If it gets too bad, we'll operate to relieve the pressure. In the meantime, we just have to wait." The doctor flicked through images on his iPad.

"What are his chances of waking up?"

"I can't tell you that right now," the doctor answered, his eyes darting up to hers and then back down. "It's touch and go."

I'm not going to wake up, Morgan, Tim told her. *I know it. You're going to have to take care of Timmy without me.* She looked at him and saw a tear slip down his cheek.

Morgan looked at the doctor and looked back at Tim.

Visions played through her mind of years of reluctant visits to a disgusting nursing home visiting her mostly dead husband. She imagined his voice living in her head, telling her what an awful parent she was.

The baby let out a little whimper.

She knew what to do. It was for the best. It wouldn't be right to leave Tim in this bed to rot. And the baby…well. She would do what she had to do about the baby.

She nodded at the doctor and he left, giving her a squeeze on the shoulder but still not looking up from his iPad. Morgan peered around the room for a place to put the baby that wouldn't get her yelled at. At a loss for another location, she laid him on the floor, over by the wall so she wouldn't step on him. He started crying again and she nudged him with her foot.

"Shush," she said. "Give me a minute."

She turned to the bed.

Did you seriously just put an infant on this filthy floor? Morgan!

"I have a choice," she said to herself as she worked one of the thin pillows out from under Tim's head. She pushed it down over his face, leaning her weight onto it.

"You shouldn't have to live like this," she murmured soothingly, although her actual thought was, *I'm not going to live like this.*

Morgan? What are you doing? Stop!

She ignored Tim's voice in her head and found the green digits that showed his oxygen level. They weren't budging. His chest continued pumping up and down.

"Dammit," she muttered, realizing what was wrong. "Idiot." Tim was intubated.

A machine was breathing for him. She wasn't going to be able to smother him.

She removed the pillow and looked at him. His face was so peaceful, although he was still yelling at her in her head. Her eyes fell on the wall socket, which was packed with cords. *Aha!*

Maneuvering her way around the bed, stepping over the baby wiggling on the floor, Morgan grasped the cords and pulled them out several at a time, gritting her teeth when the remaining machines alarmed briefly before she unplugged them too.

On the bed, Tim's back arched and he took two ragged, ineffective breaths around the tube in his throat. White foam frothed out from between his lips. His legs and arms thrashed briefly, and then he was still. She watched for a moment, but he didn't move again, and the voice in her head was silent.

Phewf.

She plugged the machines back in, waited for a moment to make sure they didn't spur him back to life, then bent down and picked up the baby up by one arm. With the other hand she collected her purse. The alarms were blaring now. Peeking both ways out the door, she saw Reonna walking quickly toward the room.

Feigning a sob, she said loudly, "I can't be here for this!" and headed for the exit.

The curly haired brunette watched her walk down the hall toward the reception desk, concern plain on her face as the baby dangled from her grip.

Morgan walked up to the desk and looked at the woman for a moment, sizing up the gentle curve of her cheeks, the smile lines by her eyes. She gave a little nod.

"He needs changing," Morgan said. "And a bottle." She held Timmy out to the woman. The baby cooed and kicked his feet.

The woman reached out for him, snuggling him with both arms. His little hand gripped her finger. Morgan rolled her eyes. "Where are you going?" the nurse asked, frowning.

"To the store and then home," Morgan answered mildly, forgetting she was supposed to be racked with grief. Her eyes fell back to the baby. "Good luck, buddy."

She smiled a little as she buckled her seat belt and drove to the Dollar Store.

There, she filled up her cart with paper plates, plastic cutlery, napkins, frozen dinners, an extra ream of printer paper, and chocolate. As an afterthought, she heaved a big bag of cat litter into the cart.

The cashier handed her a receipt. "Have a good day," he said in a bored voice.

"Thank you," Morgan said. "I will."

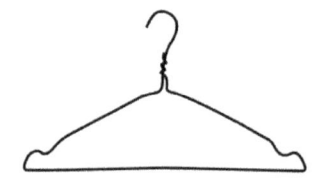

A Paring Down - Sarah Dropek

I decided I was vanishing when Veena didn't hear me ask her to add apples to the shopping list for the third time.

"I know they're not in season anymore and you're trying to be more conscious about all that, but I want to take some time this weekend to slow down and bake with you. Like we used to," I muttered when she still hunched over the counter, scrolling through her phone while eating one of last week's walnut scones.

"Veena," I said a little louder.

Nothing.

I walked over and waved my hand in front of her screen, but she didn't move.

"I'm not in the mood for jokes, Vee. If you want plum instead or something, just say so. But I'm still leaving the skin on."

I pushed her shoulder playfully, hoping she would realize I was serious and pull me in for a kiss, insisting I skin the plums if I wanted anything more than a peck on the lips. But instead, she screamed like my touch had burned her. Her phone flew out of her hand and hit my face as she jumped back from me to the other side of the kitchen.

"Ow," I said, clenching my cheek.

"What the fuck, Gen?" Veena yelled, her chest heaving under the scarf she wore because she insisted on not turning the heater on until it hit sixty-seven degrees inside. It drove me crazy to be freezing in my own apartment, but I couldn't deny we needed the money. I grabbed her coffee mug that had gone cold like everything else in the place and pressed the ceramic to my cheek.

"What do you mean, 'what the fuck'?" I screeched. "*You're* the one who was pretending to ignore me."

"I wasn't ignoring you," she shook her head in confusion. "You weren't here and then you… you were right next to me. What the hell just happened?"

"You mean you didn't see me come in from the bathroom just now? Ask for apples on the shopping list? Plum pie? Nothing?"

She shook her head and a cold shiver trilled down my spine that wasn't because of the frigid apartment.

Anyone else might brush the moment off as a fluke of one sort or another.

But I couldn't. Not after my shower this morning. She usually jumped in to harmonize with my off-key singing while we got ready for work, but this morning I sang a solo. I thought the asshole from our subway ride the night before must still have had her in a funk. She always took a little longer than me to recover from the bigots who couldn't handle us holding hands. And the old lady last night had been in a fit over me just leaning my head on Veena's shoulder. So I had belted out the chorus from her favorite childhood movie trying to cheer her up, but she still hadn't chimed in.

And now I knew it's because she had never heard me at all. Because I was disappearing. That I was sure of. I just didn't know why, how, or what would happen if I got to a point where I didn't reappear.

Veena must have seen the fear that settled like ice in my bones because she closed the gap between us quickly and replaced the mug I held against my cheek with her hand.

"I can get apples," she whispered, then offered me a tentative smile. "And splurge on some fancy candles so we don't have to smell 5b smoking every freaking Friday for a few weeks."

I gave her a weak laugh in return. She sweetly tucked a curl behind my ear that would no longer stay in my bun after I'd given in to her begging and let her cut my hair. I almost believed everything would be fine, that we'd figure out the mess of me vanishing together. But then she leaned in and kissed me in a way that felt as foreign as the idea that I was disappearing, and I wanted to yank back from her.

It was like her lips knew what her brain could not accept, and they tasted me with hesitation, with an uncertainty Veena had never had before about anything.

"Hey," she murmured when I pulled away, "I'm sorry. I wouldn't ever—"

A knock sounded at our door, and she blew out a breath of frustration. I drank in her scent of coffee and sweet honey as if it could fix everything, flinching when she shoved the deadbolt free.

"You ladies alright in here?" came the familiar drawl of 5b.

I pasted on a smile and joined Veena so she wouldn't have to deal with him by herself. I might be fading to nothing, but I'd talk to 5b for as long as I had left so Veena didn't have to do it alone. That, and I was always worried if I let her be too mean to him, he'd find something asinine to complain to management about and get us evicted.

"Heard some yelling and wanted to check on ya," he said, shooting me a half-cocked smirk that made my skin crawl.

5b was in his usual uniform of workout clothes that looked painted onto his muscular frame along with his collection of tattoos that wrapped around his arms. Reaching up to grab his cigarette revealed the long legs of a prosaically busty brunette who graced his bicep, and I fought the urge to visibly cringe. He blew some smoke from his thin, hand-rolled cigarette into our entryway. I clenched Veena's hand.

"We're good, thanks," I said. "Just burned myself a little on—"

"We're fine," Veena snapped, her nostrils flaring at the smell of the smoke before she slammed the door in his face.

"It doesn't hurt to be nice," I said to her as his laugh echoed from the hall, not helping his cause at all.

"Doesn't it?" she asked, peering at me as if I was an unknown again, some strange specimen to study. Her head cocked to one side and her eyes narrowed.

"You would let him walk all over you if it weren't for me," she hissed. "It's the only reason you're with me. Little Gennifer won't ever stick up for herself. Let Veena be the bad guy so everyone will still like you. Why are you so desperate for his approval?"

My thoughts faltered at the slap of her words, and I opened my mouth, only to close it again. A serene smile skated across her face as if she had just won a game I hadn't known we were playing. I wrapped my arms tightly around myself.

"Vee—"

"I'll go to the store after work tomorrow," she promised, suddenly back to herself again like she hadn't just sliced me in two.

"Okay," I said slowly, deciding then that I couldn't tell her I was disappearing, not when it seemed like that might be what she wanted most of all. "Thank you."

"Don't thank me yet," she grinned, giving me a kiss on the cheek as she grabbed her dance bag. "I'm gonna make you skin those apples. Someday you'll admit the pie gets bitter if you leave them on."

"Can't make it too sweet when your lips are already sugar," I mumbled the words I knew she was expecting, and she opened the door to leave for her rehearsal.

I wondered if she noticed that I didn't sound the same, or if it was that she hadn't heard me at all.

#

The kitchen felt haunted after Veena left. Her harsh words hovered around me, pressing in like the cold always did if I stood still for too long. I felt their poison as waves of chills over my skin and wondered if I was invisible now because of them. I wondered, even as my breath squeezed in my chest with the thought, if it was Veena vanishing me. It wouldn't have been the first time someone didn't want me anymore but couldn't find a way to tell me.

And that pain of rejection was something to grab on to, even if the thorns of it bit at my heart. It was something understandable where my vanishing was not. I breathed out and tried to imagine my exhale pushing Veena's jabs away from me, and I left. Because as much love that I had for Veena, I couldn't let myself disappear for it.

I didn't know where I was going when I stepped out into the hall, but I didn't have to decide when 5b spotted me as he opened his door for a pizza delivery. For the first time, his pale brown eyes seemed to hold a little kindness for me, and he nodded his head for me to come over.

I smiled at the woman who had delivered his pizza as I passed her.

"I love your hair," I said, looking at the blue streaks threaded through her dirty blonde curls.

She said nothing back and I froze in the hallway, unsure if she simply wasn't very friendly, or if I didn't exist to her.

"Coming in for a slice or what?" 5b said to me, and I tried to shake off the fear that I had already faded away for good.

"Yeah. Thanks," I said. "I'm sorry about earlier by the way. I know Veena isn't always overly nice when—"

"Not in her nature to be," he said with a shrug and a smile.

I didn't want to agree with him, so I laughed a little in reply, even though it still felt like a betrayal.

He moved from his doorway, and I walked into his sparse apartment, shedding my coat as I defrosted in the warmth. He had every requisite piece of furniture, but you could hardly call the place homey. Weights, resistance bands, and cushioned mats took up about half the living space and the only thing that decorated the walls were taped up circuit training workouts in long lines of computer paper. It made the place look like an oversized prison with white bars that locked him inside.

"Do you mind? It's cheat day," he said, and I looked back to see him holding a cigarette in the air.

"No, it's fine," I said. "Your place, go for it."

He laughed as he struck a match, shaking his head.

"Doesn't it suck that you can't be that chill with her?" he asked, his words blowing out little plumes of smoke.

"What do you mean? This is how I always am," I said, instantly annoyed at myself for coming in here and proving Veena right that there was some sick part of me that wanted this guy to like me even when, at his best he was a patronizing chauvinist, and at his worst, he was a straight up asshole.

He sat down and put a paper plate in front of the seat across from him before getting to work filling a fresh rectangle of paper with more tobacco. I watched his fingers carefully rub the paper back and forth, pressing the cigarette into shape. The crinkling sound grated my already frayed nerves, so I jumped a little when he asked if I was ever planning on sitting down. My manners had me pulling out the chair even though all I wanted to do was leave. I opened the pizza box. Meat lovers. Of course.

"See, you say this is how you always are," he began, taking a drag of his fresh cigarette, "but I know before you met her, you wouldn't have looked at that pizza like I got it out of the dumpster. Why don't you let it be a cheat day for us both, huh?"

He blew out the rest of his smoke and grabbed a slice. I started to get up from my chair, thanking him for the invitation and muttering something idiotic about the merits of vegetarianism when my eyes snagged on his smoke cloud moving over my hand. As it dissipated into the air, my hand seemed to disappear with it. I flicked my wrist to the side and saw myself again. I wanted to believe it was a trick of the light, but the only trick was that 5b had lured me in here to begin with. I ran from his apartment, breathing again only after I had double locked myself back into my cold cave.

#

Veena came home sweaty and smiling from rehearsal. But when she dropped her bag by the door, her smile dropped with it when she looked up and noticed me sitting on the counter waiting for her.

"Why do you smell like smoke?" she asked, her voice cracking around the words.

I set down the bowl of soup I had been nursing, grateful at least to know she could see me for now.

"Veena, I think I'm disappearing," I began before it all spilled out too fast for me to even try to sound like I wasn't losing my mind. "And not metaphorically. Like honestly vanishing so that you can't see me sometimes and I think you're doing it because something is wrong between us, but you don't want to say. And I don't know how you're doing it or when or why it happens, but I don't want to go, not if we can fix this. I love you. I want to fix it. Whatever it is."

Veena gave a bark of a laugh and looked at me like I had slaughtered the animals for 5b's pizza myself.

"You have really lost it, haven't you, Gen?" she said. "Listen, the door's open. I don't want to be the whipping girl for your insecurities anymore. If you feel like you're disappearing, maybe it's because you've lost yourself trying to please everyone all the time. Laughing at 5b's backhanded jokes, desperately holding my hand one second only to drop it the next because you're so afraid of what people will or won't think of you. I'm done playing my part in your exhausting game."

Veena reached into her dance bag and dropped some groceries on the counter as she stalked past me to our room. Hot tears seared down my freezing cheeks as I turned and rifled through them. There were candles and my favorite conditioner I only ever got on sale. And there was a bag with six honeycrisp apples and another with almost a dozen plums.

My teeth chattered as I stared at the fruit, willing it to make any sort of sense when Veena came back. She held her phone at her ear while her other hand clenched her scarf, and she paced the short length of our living room.

"Carmen, have you seen Gen?" Veena begged our friend.

I waited, barely breathing, for the inevitable answer. Because of course Carmen hadn't seen me. And Veena couldn't now, either. Veena slumped onto the couch and held her forehead in her hand as Carmen replied.

"I don't even really know," Veena explained into the phone, beginning to sniff back tears. "I think we had a fight? I can't explain it, Carmen. I know Gen's gone. I know it's my fault. But I can't remember anything I said. It's like I blacked out when it happened or something, but I'm—no, I'm fine, it's just…Listen, call me if she shows up at your place. Please."

She said thank you and hung up before she let out a frustrated scream, kicking the coffee table with her boot. She cried harder and frantically tapped out a text that vibrated my phone on the counter. I didn't dare pick it up, but felt my panic rise as I read the beginning of a long apology before the phone turned back to black.

It hadn't been Veena spitting cruelty at me. It wasn't her making me vanish.

"Veena!" I screamed. "Vee, please see me!"

When she didn't react at all, I poured the apples from the plastic bag and swept them off the counter. Their heavy thuds were drowned out by her piercing shriek.

"Veena, I'm here. I know you didn't mean any of it!" I yelled, pulling a ripe plum out and squeezing it in my fist.

Veena went deathly still.

"Please. Please don't hurt me," she begged quietly, her eyes locked to where the plum juice dripped from my elbow to the floor.

"You'll only scare her to death with a display like that," I heard from behind me.

I dropped the plum and Veena whimpered as I turned to see 5b leaning against our fridge, a cigarette hanging loosely in his lips.

"Don't worry," he said, "she can't see either of us right now."

I looked to the plume of smoke he blew out above his head, then back at Veena crying silently in the corner.

"Your little outburst with the fruit, anything you hold or move, will be visible and terrifying to her. But the magic that turns her mind, this bit of smoke?" he smiled at his cigarette held gingerly between two fingers. "It's as invisible as you are."

I watched the gray cloud vanish into the air and seethed.

"What are you doing to her?" I demanded, swiping tears from my face. "What are you doing to *me*?"

"I hoped you'd come to your senses on your own," he said with a laugh as if he should have known better. "But it seems she rubbed off on you and made you too hard-headed."

"What do you mean, come to my senses?" I demanded.

He smiled and sighed like he was dealing with a reluctant child, rubbing a hand over the manicured scruff of his face.

"I've watched you trying so hard to be like her," he said, walking to where I was backed against the counter. "But it was stealing everything beautiful about you, Genny. Like this damn haircut she gave you, how thin you are after eating all her weird vegan shit. I know it's not you. I know you'd rather be with me, with a real man instead of all that pretend she likes to play with her flannels and Carhartt crap. I know you'd rather have me even if you—"

"You don't know anything about me," I spat. "What the fuck did you do to her to make her be so mean? Why can't she see me?"

He laughed, reaching up to play with a lock of my hair, "Not just her, sweetheart. Everyone. Unless you stick with me, you go poof."

I looked back to the corner where Veena had been that was now empty and found her slowly coming out from our room with a bag in hand. She took a deep breath, her lower lip shaking in fear, before dancing over and around the mess of apple and plum to the door, fleeing whatever ghost she thought I had been.

When I looked back to 5b, his smirk became a confident grin.

Like someone used to getting what he wanted, he thought he'd won, tricking Veena into pushing me away and then giving me an ultimatum to stay with him or vanish. He thought he knew me. And in a way, I guess he did. Because I *was* desperate to be seen. I always had been. It's why I let Veena cut my hair even though I was excited for it to grow out. And it's why I bit my tongue and smiled when someone told a shit joke, even when it was at my expense. I wanted people to see me as more than just one thing, more than the box their brain tried to put me in. But 5b's little game of smoke taught me so clearly how wrong I had been. I saw finally that more than wanting to be understood, or even to be seen at all, I wanted to *be*, without overthinking it to death for once in my life.

I put on my best and most practiced smile, stepped over the fruit of pies that would never be made, and walked with him to his apartment.

His arrogance made it all too easy to put on a convincing show, a performance I'd been putting on forever in one way or another anywhere I went.

I made like I was grateful to him all evening. I fawned over all the shit he wanted to talk about the onslaught of 'progressive political crap.' I promised in the morning to make him all of the pies he'd been smelling for years from our apartment. I laughed with him about how he'd make himself sick eating even just a slice from each. Then I went to the bathroom before bed and tucked his straight razor into the waist of the pants he'd lent me to sleep in. And then I slit his throat while he snored with his heavy arm draped over me. As he bled out, I felt my disappearance solidify in my body in one final cold shiver. Sadness settled in my chest knowing Veena would never see me again. But even with that weight, I couldn't contain my relief at finding my greatest fear could also be my greatest freedom.

Because invisible people don't get caught for murder. Invisible people don't need to worry that their hair is drenched in blood, or that they might be seen by cameras leaving the apartment of a dead man. And they certainly don't worry about how others will see them or what they will think of them. Because they aren't seen at all. But I would make sure at least Veena thought of me, even if it was only one last time. I would make sure she understood that it wasn't her fault.

So I took my time. I dragged 5b into his living room and made my cuts precise as I peeled his tanned and tattooed shell from his sculpted muscles.

Peaches gave up their flesh so easily under a knife, and the first tear into a perfectly ripe banana could give me goosebumps with the satisfying shushing sound of the peel pulling away from itself. But I was sweating by the time I realized I wouldn't be able to lift 5b by myself. I had to settle for flaying him open wherever I could reach and hoping that when Veena came looking for me, she would see him and know I had done it. And she would understand that I would never leave the skin on again.

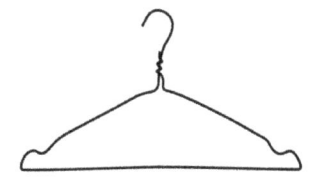

Urban Forestry- Maureen O' Leary

I was at work when I read that two homeless women were found mauled on the river trail, one to death and partially eaten. It was enough to make me forget my empty belly for a minute. The year before, seven homeless women were murdered in their camps by the river, so destroyed that the cops first thought of packs of stray dogs or urban coyotes. But no. The killer's DNA was human. I'd been following the story on my true crime video channel when the Riverside Killer went dormant. His return could be my big break.

    I personally knew a couple of the victims, because before my job at the store, I knew what it was like to sleep in a room with twenty other snoring women in a church basement. When the shelter spaced filled I headed for the river with the other turnaways, hiding in the trees and hoping to make it through the night.

Now I could afford the weekly rate at the Del Mar Motel for a room with a hot plate and a deadbolt. I was building a true crime video channel telling stories of murdered women, and though advertisers paid me a few cents per viewer I didn't have enough of those yet to make any real money.

At the end of my shift I went back to the floor. I always made sure I worked an extra fifteen minutes off the clock the days I helped myself to a cup of noodles from aisle twenty-two. At the end of the month I never had any cash for food and that day I was so hungry I was lightheaded.

At the end of the aisle, my boss intercepted me with a hand on my elbow. In his office he had me on security camera stuffing the noodles into my pocket. He didn't care that I worked extra on the days I stole food. He fired me and told me to leave, my work vest and my dinner left behind on his desk.

I pedaled away from the store, the bald tires squeaking before I got my speed up. Without a paycheck, I wouldn't have rent when it came due. I turned toward the river, the wind cooling my stinging face on the downhill. If I spent the next few days devoted to my true crime channel I could get the Riverside Killer video up by the weekend. Maybe I would get enough hits to buy time until I got another job. I had to try.

The body of the dead woman was in the morgue. The woman who escaped was named Delanie and she was in serious condition at Sutter General. I would see if I could talk to her later, but first I needed solid footage of the river.

There was a police in uniform on the riverbank when I got there, standing over a patch of grass cordoned off by yellow tape. He didn't see me approach as he spouted an arc of urine onto the crime scene. I recognized him by his ginger buzz cut and thick neck. Officer Don Bradley used to come through the shelter with a narcotics dog, arresting women with drugs in their stuff. I straightened my shirt, hoping I wasn't smelly. I didn't want him to have a reason to look down on me.

I pretended to ignore him zipping up his fly and turned to take my video.

He came up on me so fast and close I could smell *him*, his baloney on white bread smell. "Hey," he said. "Don't I know you?"

I stood my ground even as my knees turned to water. He took my chin between his fingers and squeezed the bone as if he recognized the stink of a woman with no family, no money, no real home.

I didn't answer and when he let go of me I ran away, afraid to look back, expecting at any second to feel his hands on my neck. At the shelter last winter he returned one woman the same night he took her. I didn't remember her name but she cried until morning, her back to the rest of us in the drafty common room. The next day her arms, neck and even her face were covered in bloody bite marks.

But Officer Don wasn't interested in following me. I could be grateful at least for that small favor. I was exhausted and hadn't eaten in over a day, but I was hopped up on adrenalin and ready to visit the hospital. I had this idea that if I kept moving I wouldn't have time to be freaked out over getting fired, over the rent, over being hungry.

At Sutter General the nurse let me through with just an ID and a claim to be Delanie's sister. She left me in the room where tubes and wires connected a thin woman under a blanket to a line of softly beeping machines. A stench of piss came off her in a wave as thick as incense. She was sleeping, her jaw slack and her mouth an empty hole except for two rotten pillars jutting from her bottom gums. Dirt packed her fingernails and streaked her swollen knuckles. Dried blood and other fluids stained the swath of gauze covering her neck and shoulder. Indeed she was familiar from the shelter. Delanie was the woman Officer Don brought back weeping and bitten but I could not get lost in sympathy and regret. I needed video.

She grunted awake, her eyes yellow where they should have been white. She strained to see out the window. "Is it night time yet?" she asked in a whisper.

"Not yet," I said. It felt wrong taking my phone out to film but I needed the hits on my channel. I turned on my phone and pressed record.

Delanie tapped a blackened fingernail against the metal bed rail. "I have to get to the river," she said. She yanked the tube out of her nose and pulled the IV tape from the back of her hand.

"Who did this to you?" I asked.

She whipped her head around and swung her legs over the side of the bed. I held my phone between us like a shield. She smiled and where before there had been mostly gums, there were now two full rows of teeth that looked filed sharp.

My heart pounded in my ears. My backs of my knees turned to water from the pure adrenalin born of panic. But I didn't leave. I stood transfixed even as she moved toward me, the dirty gauze covering her neck oozing red in a growing nimbus. I stood paralyzed like a rabbit who thinks that if she just stays still, she will live.

Delanie's mouth clamped on my forearm and she wrenched my skin between her teeth. Pain shot into my armpit as she popped up, grinning at me with my blood streaking her teeth. My head floated from my neck on a silken thread and I blacked out on my way to the floor.

I awoke in a bed behind a hospital curtain, my empty stomach seizing. I had to eat. I had to get outside. I couldn't afford even an hour in a hospital bed. The fluorescent bulbs buzzed under my skin and I couldn't breathe. My backpack was on the floor by my shoes, along with my cell phone. I slipped out of the automatic doors into the cool evening, the air hitting my face and tasting unbearably sweet. My arm throbbed under a bandage and I hoped a doctor gave me a tetanus shot while I was unconscious. If the bite got infected I would be screwed, but as badly as it hurt, Delanie biting me gave me an edge on my channel. I rode to the river even though the bruised sky was turning dark. The danger would be another edge, making the episode even better.

Once on the riverbank, I knelt behind the crime scene tape. The ground was redolent with the scent of the dead woman's struggle and her blood. Officer Don's urine. The smell of his boots.

Behind me women rustled amid the urban forestry, watching from the branches. Some huddled in burrows under twisted roots, chewing on dry fennel stalks that grew by the water for the sweet foamy marrow that numbed their hunger. These were women who hid from cops, abusive boyfriends, husbands and strangers. I sniffed the air for the ozone of their terror and sadness.

In the distance a car door slammed. Despite the darkness I had no trouble seeing Officer Dan chugging toward me until he raised a flashlight and blinded my vision. He was on me, cracking his baton across the backs of my knees, moving too fast for me to do anything but fall.

The ground smelled of loam and earthworms and the dead woman's body, yes, and also the smell of a male with skin that reddened in the sun. It wasn't just his pee and his boots, there was his sweat, his need, and the small bits of him she scratched away in the struggle for her life.

"It's you," I said, my voice low and unfamiliar to myself.

Officer Don jumped on my back and played his teeth against the apple of my cheek. I pushed against him but he was a hulking beast. I screamed and the sound was guttural and strange. Another scream answered from down the river in a voice like mine, female and full of rage. At the sound, Officer Don leapt off me. A dark outline of a creature came toward us in the moonlight but she was not a woman. She was on all fours. She growled from deep within her throat.

I crawled away toward the trees, my throat burning as if laced with spines. A night wind whooshed through branches. My ears pricked to the sighs of the women watching. Sheltered under a willow tree, I watched as Officer Don pulled his shirt off. His hulking shoulders popped with long bristled hairs and his tongue hung out from between a line of enormous teeth. He faced the other, smaller wolf. Her scent blew towards the trees. It was Delanie. A whine escaped my throat that didn't sound like my voice or like the voice of any human woman. I ran my tongue over my own teeth and they were sharp.

Officer Don circled her. Above me in the branches, a woman cursed.

"He's going to kill her for real this time," she said. "And then who will look after us?"

She clutched a blanket about her shoulders and she smelled of menstrual blood, peach body spray, and the small acid hope that maybe things would be okay.

Officer Don lunged at Delanie and clamped his jaws on her shoulder. At her howl I bounded from under the tree. Not thinking. Not afraid. My heart bursting with love for Delanie, for the girl in the tree, for the dead women, for every woman behind every pair of eyes glittering in the urban forest. I darted through the darkness and rammed my snout into the soft place between Officer Don's hind legs and ripped it open with my fine teeth. As the fur shed from his pink skin and his face flattened into a dying man's, I licked his blood and found it delicious.

    Delanie nudged my side and I followed her down the shoreline. We would guard the urban forest by the river. We would make safe the women in the trees holding on to the small hope that they would be okay if they could only survive one more night alive.

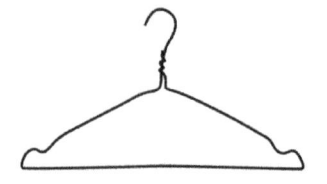

The Quantum Mixtapes of New Venus- Joan Wendland

I was next up in the librarian pool. Fresh off of a vacation I was ready to jump back into the game – until the bell rang and I got a look at my destination. The rest of the pool moaned in sympathy.

"I didn't even know they had a library on that station," said Charles.

"Neither did I," I said as I stood up and grabbed my satchel. "I just hope librarians are men there. The last thing I want to do is be a woman on New Venus."

A chorus of amens arose as I made my way to the portal.

***

I popped out behind a young boy. He was too young to cause me any trouble, but I was still nervous about being on New

Venus, so I took a moment to look down and see if I was male or female here.

Oh, damn it to hell. I'm a woman on a pleasure station. I hope to God I'm not attractive. My best course of action is getting the boy his information and get back to base as quickly as possible.

"May I help you, young sir?" came out of my throat with a quaver.

My voice didn't just sound nervous; it sounded old. Like, granny old. What a relief! The boy had jumped half out of his shoes when he heard me behind him. He whirled to face me with frantic eyes like a startled deer. I waited for him to register I was just a harmless old lady, but he remained spooked.

Something was off here. Even a young boy on New Venus should be showing some swagger. Why was he afraid of her unless…oh. On closer inspection what I have here is a girl dressed up as a boy. My best guess in the ten to twelve range. Just shy of a working girl in this amoral tin can. No wonder she was so jumpy.

In an attempt to calm her, I doubled down on my apparent ignorance. "Forgive me for surprising you, young sir. May I help you find something?"

"I…I hope so," stammered the girl. "I read a book once about a girl that set fires and –"

I interrupted her, "You mustn't set fires on a space station! You could kill everyone on it!"

The child shook her head vehemently, "No, no! I just meant, I mean in the book it says if you don't know what to do ask a librarian."

I relaxed a hair. "Sound advice. I'm sorry to have misunderstood you. What do you need to know?"

She looked about anxiously. Whatever it was she wanted to ask, she clearly didn't want to be caught doing it. I looked around myself and spotted a door marked 'Employees only'.

"Why don't we go into my office?"

***

The girl looked less frightened once I got her off the main floor. I coopted the first office I came to and closed the door. I took the chair behind the desk, and she stood beside the visitor's chair shifting from foot to foot. I was reminded of a wild animal approaching a picnic – both wanting the food, and wanting to flee.

"Please sit down, dear. I'm not going to give you away."

She froze in place and stared at me with panicked eyes.

"Really, I'm here to help. By the looks of things, you don't have a lot of time left before you're pressed into service. Let me help you."

She gasped, "It's just like in the book! I don't want to be caught, but I don't know what to do!"

I nodded sympathetically. "Well you've come to the right place. Why don't you sit down and tell me your story from the beginning?"

The girl practically fell into the chair. She looked like she wanted to cry, but held it together.

"Momma wants to get us off the station before I…before I get too grown up. She's been saving money ever since I was born, and she finally has enough to buy two tickets on the shuttle, but they won't sell them to her! They say they're full, come back next trip. But they're always full!"

I sighed, "Oh honey, you know they're not always full, don't you?"

She looked down at her hands, and I saw a tear make its way down her cheek. "Momma says they don't want her to leave 'cause she's still pretty. But by the time she's old…" The girl lost her emotional battle and began to cry. Who could blame her?

I got up and came around to put a comforting hand on her arm. I crouched down to her level and she threw her arms around my neck and bawled her heart out.

I waited until it was over except for some hiccups, then got down to business.

"You need a different way off the station, and I'm going to help you find one."

Big watery eyes looked up at me in despair. "How?"

I gave her a reassuring smile and recited the librarian's mantra, "There's no better way to start than with a book."

I reached into my satchel and pulled out a battered trade paperback titled, 'Cyphers, Steganography, and Secrets: A Complete History of Hidden Messages'. I don't know what I was expecting, but it sure wasn't this. Still, the satchels are rarely wrong, so I turned to the table of contents. On its second page I found what we must need - 'The Quantum Mixtapes of New Venus' on page 355. I turned to the chapter and began to read out loud.

"In the late twenty-second century, the women of Earth embarked on an ambitious project. Much like abolitionists of the nineteenth century, the Mixologists wanted to create a pathway to free the women of New Venus. While technically not slaves, the women of New Venus were essentially trapped on the notorious pleasure station with very few ways to earn a living – all unpleasant. The only profession that could keep a woman out of poverty was prostitution – which legally could be pursued by children as young as thirteen."

The child sniffled, and I paused to reassure her.

"Don't worry. These Mixologists sound like just what you need. Let me see what the book says about them."

I scanned through, but did not read aloud the draconian restrictions women faced on New Venus. The communications blackout for women ran both ways - no messages in, no messages out. Women weren't allowed access to news feeds either. They were only permitted music and novels from the eras before space travel. These were the vehicles that the Mixologists exploited.

"Listen! This is the important part! The Mixologists sent doctored monofilament audio tapes to New Venus with secret messages hidden on them! If you put them into a player correctly, you only heard music, but if you plug them in upside down you can hear how to escape!"

I looked at the child expecting excitement, or at least a little hope, but she was shaking her head with a frown.

"You can't plug in a mono tape upside down," she said. "The player won't let you. There's holes on the casing on the right side."

I smiled at that. "Well, then. That will make it easy for us to find one of these quantum mixtapes. All we have to do is find one with holes on both sides."

***

We spent the next hour combing through the library's extensive collection of music. I chatted with the girl to keep her spirits up. After an hour or so she unbent enough to tell me her name was Tanner because her mother had started up the fiction that she'd had a son from the day her daughter was born.

I told Tanner about all the jobs women could have back on Earth. She was stunned to learn women could be doctors, or pilots, or even police. Spurred on by these glittering possibilities, Tanner searched all the harder. Therefore, it was no surprise that she was the first one to find a quantum mixtape.

The tape was labeled, 'Women Sing the Blues - Various'. I had to applaud the Mixologists. There was very little chance a male visitor would visit the library at all, and even if one did, he would be unlikely to want to hear women singing about being unhappy. There was almost no chance men would stumble across the scheme. On the other hand, unhappy women would be attracted to such a tape, and they would have a fifty/fifty chance of hearing the secret message when they plugged it into a player.

Tanner wanted to try it right away, but the library didn't have any players. I helped her check the title out, then walked with her to her quarters. Tanner shrank into herself trying to look shorter as we passed strip joints, whore houses, and massage parlors interspersed with casinos and dive bars. What a dreadful place to grow up!

When we got to Tanner's quarters, we found her mother painting on her work face. She looked tired. Defeated, really. I felt a warm glow knowing I held the key to her freedom in my hand.

"Who's your friend, Tanner?" she asked.

Tanner bounced up and down in her excitement. "She's a librarian, Mom! She helped me find a tape with a secret message on it!"

The woman looked doubtful. "What secret message?"

I felt for the poor woman. "I know you don't have any reason to trust me, but we found a book in the library that says we can find you and Tanner a way off the station if we find and play the message. It's worth a try anyway. Can we use your player?"

Tanner's mother moaned in misery. "Lady, don't get Tanner's hopes up."

"Please, Mom! Pleeeease!" begged Tanner.

"It'll only be music, but I don't mind music."

***

We put the tape in, and a soulful woman sang about washing dirty sheets. Not even her own sheets, but someone else's.

"Told you," said Tanner's mom as she reached for her hairspray.

I popped the tape out and flipped it around. This time there was no music. A woman spoke slowly and carefully with precise enunciation.

"Women of New Venus, there is a way off station for you. Say, 'Little boy blue, let me blow your horn' to any of the following sympathetic pilots: Yancy Theodore of the freighter Gentleman Cowboy, Malloy Holmes of the currier Sea Biscuit, and Hodgell Harper of the miner Smashomatic. These men will be wearing a patch with a blue martini glass somewhere on their uniforms. They will be your guides off-station. Good luck to you."

All three of us stared at the player as the message repeated. On the third repetition Tanner's mother recited the code phrase along with the tape. By the fourth repetition, her tears had ruined her makeup. She wiped it off and began reapplying it, but she didn't look tired anymore.

Cuckoo- Kay Hanifen

They call us the town of little miracles. One day, a comet flew overhead, and all fully grown people with uteri of reproductive age woke up three months pregnant. Before we could seek abortions, the state swooped in and quarantined us. Apparently, we were too "scientifically significant" to have bodily autonomy. They wanted to study the parasites put into us and see whatever inevitably comes bursting out in a shower of blood and viscera. Of course, they'll provide us with the utmost care until they're born.

So, I've been trapped at this facility for four months feeling this…thing grow and move inside me, watching my body balloon into something unrecognizable. All the nurses here act like it's just a normal pregnancy and ask me what I want to name it or if I hoped it was a boy or a girl.
Like I wasn't just raped by the universe.

And yesterday, they arrived. At the same time, we all went into labor. They said the births were unusually easy. Some minor cramps no worse than a period, some pushing, and the squalling creature was out. Those who had given birth before agreed that this was far less painful than their previous children. But I hadn't even had sex before that day, so I had no point of reference. All I know is that I pushed something out of my body, something that hurt in the leadup and exit like I was being torn in half. Then they pressed on my stomach, trying to expel the extra blood and gunk after passing the placenta. It was supposed to be a massage, but it hurt far more than it relaxed, forcing my uterus to contract and shrink.

Now I'm sitting in adult diapers so that I don't bleed or piss all over the hospital bed while the creature I gave birth to is suckling at my tits. "It's a girl," they said, as though that should make me happy. As though it didn't seal away its future should this happen again.

I don't even want to call it a girl. The government is breathing down our necks trying to get us to sign away our rights as parents so that they can turn these things into little lab rats, and I think I might do it. If I start calling it a girl, thinking of it as mine, then I'm scared it will make the decision to leave it harder.

I don't want it. I never did. But as much as I loathe what's been done to me—the tearing, the stretching, the morning sickness, and swollen breasts—I'm still human. Abortion is one thing. Blocking some hormones and expelling a clump of cells. It would have felt nothing. But this is a living creature now and it looks at me with large silver eyes far more intelligent than a newborn's should be. Now that it's here, I don't want it to suffer as a science experiment.

It lets go of my nipple, and automatically, I bring it up to my shoulder to pat its back and burp it like they taught us in those mandatory parenting classes. New parents always describe the wonderful, miraculous feeling that comes from bringing a life into this world and the beautiful bonding experience of breastfeeding. I look at this thing now asleep on my chest and I feel nothing. It's just using my body all over again without my permission. I don't even think it's all that cute. Its eyes are unnaturally large—even for an infant's—and it's wrinkly like a Shar Pei. The nurses all gush over her "widdle nosies and toesies," but to me, it doesn't look all that different from the placenta I passed.

Speak of the devil… "Knock-knock," one of the more obnoxious nurses,

Tina, says as she pokes her head in. "All done in here?"

"Yeah," I reply, sitting stock still as she picks up the creature, cooing at it like it was the cutest thing on earth.

"Have you decided what you're naming your little miracle?" she asks.

"I wouldn't call it that," I mutter as I pull up the blankets to hide my body. I just want to sleep some more before the next feeding.

Something like anger flashes across her face as she holds the infant closer, stroking its silvery hair. "You have no idea how many women have prayed to be blessed like this and would kill to be in your position."

"They can have it," I reply, wincing as I turn to face the wall, jostling my stitches, and feeling some fresh blood seep out of my ragged holes.

"Ungrateful bitch," she mutters.

Right. That's it. I sit up with a growl to hide the pain of sudden movement. "Maybe I am an ungrateful bitch, but I didn't want to be pregnant," I yell. "I've never even had sex, for God's sake! And then, one day, I wake up with this alien inside me sucking the calcium from my bones and the nutrients from my body and I'm held against my will at a hospital where I'm told that my violation is a miracle. I'm sorry if you've struggled with fertility issues, but that doesn't give you the right to criticize me for being traumatized."

Tina looksed as though she'sd been struck but saysid nothing else as she hastily makdes her escape from the room . All the while, I could can feel the silver eyes of the infant watching me. I felt feel as though I was am being judged by it and found lacking. "And fuck you too," I mutter as I flop onto the bed and turn with my back toward the door.

I wake again when someone wheels into the room. The only other queer person here, Jackson, is looking exhausted as he wheels next to me. His hair is stringy with grease, and he has dark circles under his eyes. I doubt I look much better. "Hey," I say.

He gives me a lobsided grin. "Hey. How are you holding up?"

"I'll be honest, chief, not great. Nurse Tina the Tyrant told me off for not being super enthusiastic about my post partem life and the thing that just tore through my perineum like tissue paper."

"She's the worst," he replies as he rests his chin on his hands and leans with his elbows on the side of my bed. "Four months here and she still misgenders me. What a bitch. I swear, just hearing her voice triggers my body dysmorphia." I pat his head and he falls silent for a moment, biting his lip as though he's holding back a question.

"Whatever you wanna ask, go right ahead," I say.

"Which one did you get? Boy or girl?"

"Girl."

"Boy," he says before I can ask. His cheeks color a little. "I, uh, named him Perseus."

"Perseus?" I reply, raising my eyebrows.

He awkwardly rubs the back of his neck. "I mean, we're both feeling a bit like Danae, right? Locked up and impossibly impregnated with a supernatural baby."

"Fair enough." And next is the question I'm dreading.

"Have you named yours yet?"

My jaw clenches as I brace for judgement. "No. I don't want anything to do with it. As soon as they let me out of here, I'm running as far as I can from our 'Miracle Town.' I can't be a mother to it."
He grabs my hand and gives it a sympathetic squeeze. "I get it. Really. Don't think that this makes me an enthusiastic father. I didn't even think I was going to name it, but figured I had to call it something other than my baby. Especially when I don't think of it as mine. The moment I get outta here, I'm

scheduling my top surgery, a hysterectomy, and blowing this stupid town."

"Amen to that. Gonna get my tubes tied after this. No more virgin births for me." And it's not that I hate kids. They're fine in small doses. I liked to babysit as a teenager and was the cool aunt to my nieces and nephews. But Mom and Dad love to talk about "building God's army" and the idea of having kids that become victims of that kind of manipulation is horrifying to me. The world sucks enough already. Why would I want to bring someone into this misery?

He laughs. "Man, if it turns out you gave birth to the Messiah or the antichrist, my Jewish ass is gonna kill you."

"Not if my Pentecostal parents get to me first." When they first found out about That Day, they were ecstatic that I was one of the "lucky" people blessed with a miracle and damn near killed me when I said I was going to abort it. I doubt they'll be happy that I gave it up to the government instead of letting it be raised by the church like they want.

We fall into a comfortable silence, the two of us hurting, confused, and exhausted, but enjoying each other's company. "Thanks," I say.

He blinks. "For what?"

"For being my friend. I don't think I would've survived the last few months without you."

With a wince, he slowly stands to wrap his arms around me. The hug is awkward, but it also feels good. A comforting bit of contact after days of only unwanted and clinical touches in places where I don't want to be touched. Grunting, he sits back down. "I should get back before the next feeding. Tina the Tyrant will be apoplectic if she finds out that I took the wheelchair for a joyride."

"Good luck," I reply with a laugh as he wheels off, leaving me alone once again in the hospital room. They'd done their best to make it look more like a hotel room, with soothing pink painted walls, a photograph of flowers above my head, and a television, but the bed and medical equipment are a stark reminder that this place is no vacation. Unsure of what else to do, I turn on the television.

The news is on with two reporters, male and female, smiling into the camera. "Some news from the Town of Little Miracles," the female says, "Yesterday, all seventy-four gave birth to an equal number of healthy boys and girls. No word today as to what will happen to these children, but we'll keep you updated."

"Wow Sharon, a whole town of 'Virgin Marys'. Can you imagine that?" the male says.

The female laughs. "Christmas truly came early yesterday, and what a gift indeed."

Disgusted, I turn off the television and try to sleep just a little bit more before I become a milk dispensary, but end up only staring blankly at the wall for hours.

"Knock-knock," Nurse Tina says as she carries it in to feed.

I put it on my chest, barely feeling as it latches onto my nipple and suckles. The world has become fuzzy and unreal in those intervening hours. I barely grunt as Tina leaves. My enlarged boobs ache, but it barely registers with the rest of the soreness. Once its done eating and I burp it, I let it take a nap on my chest.

But it doesn't nap. It sits staring up at me with piercing silver eyes. It doesn't cry. I didn't even hear it cry when it was born. No, it just sits and stares and people seem to know what it wants. But now it's just staring in a way I cannot begin to decipher.

"What do you want?" I ask.

It just stares.

Tears blur my vision. "What do you want? You took my body, my freedom, my sleep, my life. What else could I possibly give you?"

Its mouth slowly forms words and gurgles, unintelligible at first, but then, "Muh…muh…"

Most parents are delighted to hear their baby's first words. It's a joyful milestone for them. But hearing it call me mama pierces my heart with icy dread, and with my hormones raging I can only break down and sob. "I don't want to be your mama," I wail. "I hate you. I hate you. I hate you."

"Muh…muh…" it repeats, headbutting me with its surprising strength for a newborn. It's terrible, the temptation to just throw it across the room and be done with it, but I restrain myself. Instead, I throw down a blanket and place it on the floor for 'tummy time' while I sob. It would be easier if I loved it the way they all want me to, but every second with it makes my skin crawl. It cries with me, making me leak milk.

My body is not my own. It's been stolen from me and subject to the whims of something put into me. I don't think it will ever feel like it belongs to me again.

Nurse Tina screams when she pokes her head in and finds it on the floor and me lying with my back to it. "What did you do?"

"Tummy time," I mumble. "Don't worry. I didn't drop it."

She scoops it up and examines it just in case. "What the hell is wrong with you?"

"Call it postpartum depression," I reply. I don't care to tell her that it spoke its first words. They'll find out eventually.

"Six weeks," she mutters, "six weeks and I'll never have to deal with you again." That's how long it's supposed to take for me to be fully healed. And then I'll be dropped back into the world with some cash for the thing I carried, and a job lined up.

A lot can happen in six weeks, especially when the parasites grow at extraordinary rates. By week four, the infant is crawling and babbling. By week five, it toddles and speaks complete sentences. For some reason, they still want me to breastfeed it in case its healthy accelerated growth is caused by whatever hormones are in my body after the invasion. I think they still want us to bond with them. Some have, especially if they'd been mothers before. Even Jackson's taken to occasionally calling Perseus "lil dude" and fist bumping him. By the end of week fivefour, I'm the only one who seems to remember our violation and has refused to name it. I'm counting the days until they can let us leave.

Halfway through week five, it toddles in on its own. I keep craning my neck for Nurse Tina, but apparently the infant is an escape artist. Its silver eyes look determined as it glares up at me with far more intelligence than a toddler should have, especially considering it's actually six-weeks old and shouldn't even be able to pick up its head.

"Why don't I have a name?" it asks.

I blink, surprised by how well-spoken it is despite looking like a toddler. These things never cease to surprise me.

"Why don't I have a name?" it repeats. "Why do you keep calling me 'it'? I'm a she." She crosses her arm and stomps her foot, something that would be cute and precocious if she wasn't a five-week-old toddler.

"Sorry." It's all I can think of to say in response.

Her chin wobbles. "Why don't you like me?"

In spite of myself, my heart squeezes just a little. No one wants to be told that they're unwanted at best and their proximity is traumatizing at worst. The knowledge is a terrible burden, especially for a child. But how else do I explain to her why I can't bring myself to love her. ? I reach down and pick her up to put her in my lap. "Do you want the honest answer? It's not going to be easy to hear."

"Uh-huh." She nods, sniffling and wiping her eyes.

"The truth is that I didn't want to have you. When the comet flew overhead and I woke up pregnant, I felt scared and violated, but they made me carry you. I'm hurting, and I'm sorry I'm making you hurt too. It's not your fault." I blink, reconsidering. "I mean, it isn't your fault, right? You didn't choose to rent out my womb for whatever reason? I don't know how any of this works."

She sniffles. "No. We're the last of our kind. Our other mommies and daddies made us know everything about our world before putting us in you. I'm sorry. I didn't mean to hurt you."

I give her a squeeze and push back her silvery grey hair. It had grown to her shoulders in the past few weeks but is still soft as down. "It's not your fault that your parents hurt me."

"Do you still hate me?" she asks.

I shake my head.

"Then can I have a name now?"

Mouth dry, I nod, but come up blank. We've all had our choices ripped from us. Something drove these aliens to treat us as a Noah's ark for the last of their kind. I was forced to carry my pregnancy to term. This kid never asked for any of this to happen to her. She deserves at least make some choices. "Well, what do you want to be called?" I ask. "I think you should be allowed to pick your own name."

Her little face becomes solemn and pensive, and I find myself warming up to her just a little bit. "My other mommy was named Zella. Can that be my name?"

"Zella's a lovely name," I reply.

We fall into a comfortable silence, perhaps the first one we've had together. Surprisingly, I'm the one to break it. "You should know that I'm planning on signing away my parental rights. That means that I won't be your mom anymore in the eyes of the government."

"Oh," she says, "okay."

I'm expecting more tears and fighting on this, but she reacted in the same way she might react to learning what she'll have for dinner. "Just 'okay'?" I ask, raising my eyebrow.

She giggles. "I'm sorry, but you're not a very good mommy. You don't want to be one, and I want to belong to someone who wants me."

"Sorry I couldn't be that for you," I reply.

She shrugs and gets off the bed. When her gaze meets mine, I feel the eons of knowledge behind her eyes. "I know. Thank you for talking to me."

I watch as she toddles out the room. A week later, Jackson and I will sign away our parental rights and say goodbye to them, likely forever. We'll leave, get his gender affirming surgery, and live life on our own terms. I can only hope that someday, Zella and Perseus will have the same opportunity, but for now, I watch her disappear out the door, feeling better than I have since the day of the comet.

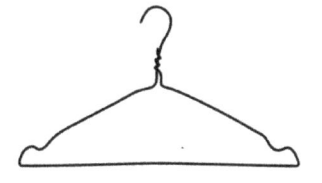

Lex Talionis - M. Edusa

Definition (noun)
lex talionis: the principle or law of retaliation that a punishment inflicted should
correspond in degree and kind to the offense of the wrongdoer; retributive justice."

.

I'm twenty-three years old and a cigarette hangs limp between two fingers, smoldering.

"What happened on August 13th," the woman across the table asks me. Her eyes are kind in that practiced and careful kind of way, like she's used to working with people. Correction: not people. Damaged children, who hear more in your body language and your tone and your face than they ever do in your words.

"I don't remember."

But that's a lie, and we both know it. I'm nine years old and the handle of the knife underneath my pillow is warm to the touch. Damp from the sweat of my palm. My fingers ache from squeezing it.

I didn't make this decision. Not consciously; actively, like you choose what shirt to wear. What color crayon to pick up out of the box, what side of the pillow to sleep on.

I didn't want to do what I had to do. Maybe the decision chose me.

We don't have beds. I'm curled up on the floor, zipped into a military green sleeping bag with a red and orange plaid design on the inside lining. I've traced every faded line, over and over with my fingers. Only with my left hand, though. My right hand has a job to do. A compulsion. A death grip.

It's early August and the single electric air conditioning unit crammed into the living room window labors loudly, struggling to cool the entire house. I imagine that I can hear the condensation dripping down the walls.

That's only in my head, though. So am I. So is the decision, the one I didn't make. The one that made me.

It's this nameless, unmade decision that guides me to peel down the sleeping bag zipper, to carefully fold back the top layer and stand on quiet, sock-insulated feet. The oscillating groans of the AC unit mask my quiet breaths. Silent footsteps. A heartbeat that has become loud enough to roar in my ears.

The tiny house sleeps in that white noise stillness. The violence sleeps.

A man I've never seen before is sitting across from me.

"Who are you," I ask him blankly, feeling nothing at all. Not even the dim curiosity new faces once inspired. Maybe that's the meds. Maybe it's just me; who I am now.

"My name is Doctor Lane, but you can call me Jasper," he answers cordially.

Jasper. It's a name I once secretly thought of as melodic, poetic, even romantic. In my brain, it now slots over into the "bad" column with a sound like a heavy gate slamming shut. Another word on a long list of all disdained and distasteful things that have become irrevocably tainted.

Sour by association. No longer reminiscent of copper-hued stones gleaming with polish, or the vague and disjointed recollection of a book I may have read once. Ruined.

"I've always hated that name," I lie as I raise my cigarette.

He ignores the comment, as psychiatrists usually do, but his pen scratches loudly in the silence.

It's a familiar sound.

"Do you know why I'm here today?"

I huff softly, and resist the urge to shake my head. I know from experience that will only invite more tireless questions, more relentless probing.

He clearly didn't expect an answer from me, so he continues to rattle off his script.

"Your primary doctor thought a change of pace might help encourage you to open up a little more. I know that you and your previous psychiatrist had… some differences of opinion."

"Is that what we're calling it?" I barely mutter the words, but of course he hears me.

"It is," he retorts cheerily, folding one leg over the other. The fabric of his perfectly-pressed slacks sounds expensive. "Unless you have another explanation."

I don't, because he's right. Something I'll never admit. Not because he's a shrink, though of course that has some bearing.

It's because I dislike him. That word isn't strong enough, though.

It's because I hate him. It's because he's a man.

That's what's really wrong with me, I know somewhere deep and hidden. That's my real
sickness. The curse of my birth. The almost-lucky dice roll of biological chance: that I was born a woman, and he wasn't. A factual inevitability so far outside of either of our control that it's absurd to assign any kind of blame to it.

I know that. I know it in my head. But that ugly, coiled-up monster in my chest doesn't give a shit.

I hate him. For the life he gets to lead so effortlessly. For the struggles he will never experience. For the ease he has, the simplicity of turning a blind eye to the ugly and inconvenient.

Silence, my only weapon, stretches between us in the clouds of cigarette smoke. I'm careful, as I've learned to be, not to smoke too fast. Not to move too much. Not to make any little furtive, anxious movements. To control my eyes and my face and my body and my voice. That's all I have, this veneer of calm. A facade, really, because it gives me the illusion of controlling something.

"What happened on August 13th?"

The question is so predictable. So tired.

"I don't remember."

It's a lie. We both know it.

"What do you remember?"

I blink slowly, slowly. Slower.

I'm nine years old and my heart is pounding as the door creaks behind me. The night air is hot and oppressive, but I'm cold. My lips feel numb.

Before this moment, in the single frantic heartbeat that exists before the knob clicks shut behind me, I never understood how a person could feel terrified and eerily calm all at the same time. I think I understand it now.

The decision I didn't make guides my footsteps in the dark. A sagging chicken-wire fence runs across a half-moon driveway, dividing the property into two: my side, the safe side, and his side.

There's an aluminum gate with a bungee-hook closure, but I know it makes too much noise. I climb over it.

His house is a sagging shack pieced together in violation of every building code of the county, and it reeks like cans of old bacon grease and cat piss. Underneath is something else;
something sour and vile that I can't put a name to. I can smell it before I reach the door, and my
stomach turns.

The three dogs sleeping on the porch raise their heads, tails thumping against the wood. Lucy and Milo and Bear. All three larger than me, all three familiar enough with my smell not to be alarmed by my presence. I hush them quietly, and they huff as their heads droop back down.

I feel sick here. Dirty and ashamed. The taste of bile rises in my throat, reminding me that this place is all wrong. My fingers shake as I touch the doorknob. It turns easily. Of course it does; he never locks his door. Out here, isolated in the endless barren desert, he doesn't think he needs to.

I creep through the dark entry, stacked high with old cabinets and gaudy curios. Crowded rows of empty cologne bottles hide behind bean pots and hideous porcelain figures. There are endless tin boxes, rusted old tools with wooden handles, vintage photos in broken frames. Dust coats every surface, clinging. Thick and stifling.

From somewhere in the adjacent room, I hear Don Knotts talking to Conan O'Brien at maximum volume. When the crowd on TV cheers, the speakers crack in distorted protest.

I'm careful to breathe through my mouth. Careful not to choke on the stench of this place. Pain shoots up my forearm, because I'm still holding that big hunting knife against my chest in a death grip, but I

don't dare relax now. The same knife I secreted away weeks ago from the old toolbox in the shed, waiting with bated breath to see if my dad would ever recognize it's
absence.

    He didn't notice. Of course he didn't. If he's home, he's angry, and drinking or sleeping or raging. Sending us kids scurrying to hide under the table when he storms through the small
house like an inferno of fury. Destroying everything in his path.

    I could have spray painted my late-night intentions in bright red, right across the front door, and he still wouldn't have noticed.

    Back in that foul-smelling house, which well into my adulthood, would come to represent everything I believed about hell, I'm still cold. Still shaking, still unwavering in my childish
determination. I peek around a towering cabinet, through the kitchen, into the small dining room.

    A single naked bulb dangles from the ceiling over a wooden kitchen table strewn with stacks of newspapers. He's sitting there with his back to me, plaid shirt, dark skin. Bent over a plate of greasy food. My grandfather.

I know I'm supposed to think of him as my grandfather, anyway, but I don't. We're not blood related, and it's easier that way. Easier to think of him as a stranger. A manifestation of the curse of my birth, hovering close, in the house next door that smells like nightmares.

To distance myself from the horror of real possibility, I tell myself that none of his blood is in my veins.

I can hear myself breathing. I can feel the spaces between every gasp speeding up, drowning out my heartbeat. I'm acutely aware that I need to find a way to slow down. If I'm going to do this, I'm going to finish it. And if I want to finish it, I need to be calm. Be still.

I press my back against the cabinet, feeling dirty, dusty hardware digging into my spine. I press until it hurts, and the mild pain distracts me.

It reminds me that my fingers hurt too. My hand and my forearm, and the bruises wrapped around my upper arm. The dark and angry ones on my hips, on my ribs. On my buttocks, my inner thighs. The pain between my legs that sometimes pierces and sometimes aches.

It's in this moment, with the clogging odor of grease and rot hanging in my nostrils; with the Late Night Show audience screaming and cheering loudly from two rooms away, that my resolve finally wavers. My grip on the knife weakens briefly. It's a heartbeat. It's a decade. Something inside me changes. Something wakes up.

"It's good to see you again," Jasper says as he shuts the door behind him.

I watch that door close, thinking about the world beyond it. I wonder how much that world has changed in fourteen years. I wonder if it's already forgotten all about me, but I think I know the answer. I think it forgot me a long, long time before I arrived here.

"I want to show you something," Jasper is saying, interrupting my wandering thoughts. I drag my eyes from the door, and now I watch as he rifles through his bag with long, bony fingers.

He's late, and I consider pointing that out. I've already burned through one of my cigarettes, and much faster than normal since there's nobody here to critique and analyze my every move. I have two more left. The hard-haggled quid pro quo of these sessions; three cheap cancer sticks. That's the price of admission.

Step right up to see the sideshow, folks: a doped-up, former child psychopath. Now an adult psychopath of course, at least according to the paperwork, and a lot less interesting to the scientific community in her old age. From adolescent killer to professional psych patient, shuffled into the void. Forgotten.

"Found it," Jasper announces at last, and I discard the temptation to remark on his tardiness.

He'd probably find some way to twist that around on me.

It's a newspaper article he sets in front of me. I glance down and see the headline through a plume of white smoke.

CALIFORNIA GIRL STABS GRANDFATHER NINE TIMES

"What's that," I deadpan. Careful, careful. Practiced apathy. Black face, blank voice. Blame it on the meds.

"You've seen this before, haven't you?" Jasper isn't thrown off by my bullshitting.

I shrug one shoulder when he pauses for an answer.

"Come on, take a look." He pushes the paper closer to me.

I tip my head at him and drop a hand onto the stack of papers. Deliberately, I push them back.

"You claim not to remember anything that happened when you were a child," he forges onward.

"I thought we might try to jog your memory."

I can feel the corner of my lip twitch and I fight back a humorless smile. I'm all too aware that such a reaction will only encourage Jasper, and cement his preconceived ideas about my mental stability. Or lack thereof.

That's part of the game. Never give them enough to make them feel like they've solved the riddle. The endless mystery of my fucked-up brain.

"Do you want to know what I think?"

"No." I blink. Slow and emotionless. It was a rhetorical; we both knew it.

Like he didn't hear me, Jasper continues. "I think you're full of shit."

Ah, the bad cop approach, I think wryly. Jasper didn't really seem like the type, but I have to respect the effort.

"I don't think you've actually repressed anything," Jasper folds his hands. "Sure, you've convinced a lot of doctors that your memory is lost, or damaged, or buried too deep to access.
But I don't really get that impression from you."

"Thank you for the insight, Doctor." I can't resist a bit of sarcastic commentary. I'm tired. So tired.

"I think you're simply avoiding thinking about it." Jasper is optimistic, persistent, even cheerful. I wonder if he's new. He's younger than most of the doctors I've seen over the years.

"How can I?" I light my final cigarette. "It's all you people talk about."

Jasper picks up the article since I won't, and starts to read aloud. "A nine-year old girl has been arrested on charges of homicide after a fatal stabbing on Thursday night, police said Friday in a news release."

I smoke, and blink. Smoke again. Shock value stopped working on me a long time ago.

"The suspect, whose name was withheld due to being a minor, was taken into custody at the scene. The victim was transported to a local hospital. However, Los Angeles Police were later informed he was pronounced dead at the hospital."

I watch the hypnotic curl of smoke, and something wild and savage stirs in my chest.

Liars, I think to myself. He was dead a long time before that.

.I'm nine years old and the monster within me is wide awake. Scratching at the walls. Pounding on it's chest, demanding release. Screaming. Salivating.

This nameless thing is an amalgamation of my childhood. It's terror and rage and indignation; it's the classic tales of revenge I used to lay awake reading all night until the sun came up. The Count of Monte Cristo, Heathcliff's furious vengeance. Artemis, seen bathing by the human Actaeon. In her fury, she turned him into a deer, and his own hounds chased him down and devoured him.

I'm thinking of that story now. I'm thinking of the dogs on the porch sleeping. The beast inside me feeds upon the thought, coaxing a glowing ember into a full-blown inferno.

The decision that made me takes control. It takes the few short steps, from behind my hiding place, to the kitchen, to the chair. I'm standing directly behind him. He's eating, and talking quietly to himself, and he's blissfully unaware that he's no longer alone.

I can taste his tongue down my throat. I can feel his big hands on my bruised skin. I can smell his heavy old-fashioned cologne, poured all over his clothes like he took a shower in it. I can feel him inside me while I cry quietly, and hear the words in my ear. Telling me over and over that this is what god wants.

In that moment, the monster gives strength to the child. Gasoline flames shoot into the night sky, and I'm powerful.

I don't know what is going to happen to me after tonight. But I know for sure, he will never touch me again.

I stab him. With all the strength in my small body, I aim between his shoulder blades, and miss. The knife sinks into the meat of his upper back, between his shoulder and his neck, and he screams. It's music to my ears.

That's right, I scream, or maybe I only think it. You should be scared of me now.

It takes a lot of effort to pull the knife out; I barely manage it before he lurches to his feet.

I don't know what he's saying. Maybe they aren't even words. Just noise.

I stab him again, this time right in the stomach, because he's towering over me. This is the last time, I promise myself, that he will ever loom above me. Dominating and terrifying me, taller than a skyscraper, darker than the shadows outside.

The Late Night Show audience jeers and screams; the speakers crackle painfully as I yank the knife out. It's easier this time. Maybe the new strength is because I can see his dark eyes, I can smell him.

Flailing, he grabs my arm. Something snaps inside me.

I blink and I'm on top of him. There's a wet squishing noise, and I'm leaning all my weight onto the knife. The silver blade has disappeared into his neck. My hands are slick with blood.

I can hear myself panting, almost hyperventilating. I can hear the tinny rattle of the speakers as the TV cuts to commercial. At the front door, the dogs are whining. Scratching at the wood.

What I can't hear is him. He's not making a single sound. Not anymore.

I push myself off his body in a rush. The thought of touching him at all disgusts me. I'm

unsteady on my feet as the adrenaline rush leaves me floating, lightheaded. My feet slide in the blood, and I catch myself on the kitchen table. Staring down at my hands. At the smeared crimson palm prints I've left next to a half-eaten plate of potatoes and steak.

I'm tempted to leave the knife where it is. I don't need it anymore.

I'm listening to Lucy howling at the door as I reach down and yank it out anyway.

I'm not finished yet.

"So in retrospect, what would you have done differently?"

The countdown reel-leader of my childhood horror cinema comes grinding to a halt. I blink, and remember where I am.

"What?" I ask distantly, like it's someone else's voice.

"Do you regret the decisions that led you here?"

Jasper's voice has that note of familiar longsuffering, poorly concealed impatience. The air of a man who's repeated himself too many times, and all the words have lost their meaning. The script has stuttered; I missed my cue. He's tired of prompting me.

Why can't she just remember her lines, he's wondering.

He came in here so convinced he could crack me, so optimistic and determined. He's irritated, now. Maybe at himself. Certainly at me.

Some twisted part of me takes a dark satisfaction in that.

"Do you regret—"

"I fucking heard you."

It's the first time I've seen a real reaction from him as he turns wide eyes to me. To be fair, it's the first time he's seen a real reaction from me, too.

I stand up. Lean across the table. I watch his throat work as he swallows, pushing himself back into his chair just a fraction of an inch. Trying not to show that he's uncomfortable.

My palm comes down onto the laminated surface, pocked and scratched and warped from the restless fingers of every

crazy woman who has ever sat in my chair, standing trial by white
walls; judgment by blue ink.

"Are you asking me if I would stab a man to death in his own home?" I say it quietly, staring into his face.

The glimmer of fear that sparks across his eyes is a rush of triumph to me. It's a fucking high. Stronger and more addictive than anything I've ever injected; it's fentanyl and heroin and
ecstasy all rolled into one, and it makes something dead in my chest sing. It's a rolling tide of
emotion and a heady reminder that I can still feel anything at all, and this might be the only way.

I stand tall over this doctor, who was lucky enough to be born a man, and watch the tables turn.

Jasper is the one with the briefcase, the steno pad, the expensive suit and stylish glasses. He can go stand at that door, push the buzzer, and all the men who run this place will let him out
the doors without question.

I'm the one who's locked in here. The one who can't have drawstrings on my clothing, can't make unsupervised phone calls. I can't take my stupid little pills without a watchful eye checking my mouth to make sure I didn't tongue them into my cheek for later.

But right now, I'm the one with the power. For a stolen heartbeat, a skip in time. In this moment, it's all mine.

"They left a lot of details out, you know," I go on, and for the first time I allow him to see that thing in me. The monster that isn't calm or rehearsed or careful. The creature that didn't fall asleep when I was nine years old, but woke up. It woke up and it roared.

"In that article." I lean closer, and the thing inside me bares it's teeth. "That little girl in California, she didn't just stab him, you know. She cut off his cock. His balls, too. Sawed them right off with a hunting knife. I wonder why they left that part out."

Further, farther, I lean in. I can smell Jasper's expensive shampoo, and see the bead of sweat on his forehead. I can watch the pulse jump in his throat.

"She fed them to the dogs," I whisper. "In retrospect, if she could have done things differently…"

I trail off, and my eyes land on his crotch. I raise a meaningful eyebrow.

I smile. "I still would have cut 'em off," I breathe, "but I think maybe I would have eaten them myself."

For the first time, Jasper has nothing to say.

The thing I see in him is a cowering animal. It's weak and soft, unaccustomed to conflict. To the struggle to survive, the war women fight to draw every single breath: breaths that aren't given and aren't earned. They're bled for.

His defeat is the death rattle of a prey animal, caught in a snare. The monster in me can almost smell it.

"So, if I could do it all again. You want to know if I would make the same decision. Knowing then what I know now. That I would end up here, locked up. Medicated. A fucking prisoner. That certifiable, professionally-diagnosed crazy bitch."

I stare at him, and he stares back, wide-eyed. This time it's my turn. My turn to push and hassle and demand an answer. He seems to sense it.

Just once, he nods.

I smile at him, and imagine that I can still taste the copper tang of blood splashing against my teeth. It's me, and it's the monster. One and the same. We both tasted blood, together. And we never felt sorry for doing it.

Slowly, I sit. Pick up my abandoned cigarette. Take a long drag.

"I would," I say to his terrified eyes. "I would do it all again in a heartbeat."

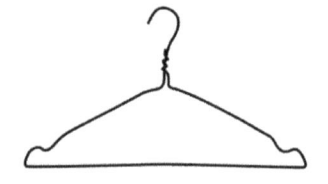

The Old Ways- Christiane Erwin

Written in response to Jonathan Mitchell, architect of Texas Senate Bill 8, aka "The Heartbeat Bill" who wrote:

Women can 'control their reproductive lives' without access to abortion; they can do so by refraining from sexual intercourse.

1

Nico headed out to the garden looking for his wife. He spotted her among the cabbage leaves, naked and sleeping. He looked her over for signs of ripeness. Unlike the small lump of flesh with no distinguishable features that had appeared months ago, she was now fully grown with black hair that flowed wild and curly.

Freckles covered the side of her body that had faced the sun. The woman was finally ready for harvesting. He grinned widely and went to fetch the wheelbarrow, somewhat chagrined that his mother had been right.

After all, his mother was the one that insisted he plant the woman seeds, having grown tired of listening to him complain about how hard it was to find the perfect wife.

"Why are modern women so needy and demanding?" he had whined to her. "All this nonsense talk of 'women's liberation.' Why can't women just be happy serving their men?"

His mother had given him a thin smile and thrust the packet of woman seeds into his hands.

"Yes, yes, there's something to be said for tradition," his mother seemed to agree. "Don't you think it's finally time you gave the old ways a try? Follow my directions, and you'll see. You'll have the perfect wife in no time at all."

Nico had been reluctant to take the woman seeds from his mother; what if he ended up with a wife that was ugly or fat? But despite his initial hesitancy, he'd followed his mother's instructions to the letter. And now, here she was, a veritable goddess, ripe and ready for picking. It had all worked out for the best.

Nico lined the wheelbarrow with blankets and rose petals and pushed it through the garden. He bent down and rolled the woman over. Her long eyelids fluttered, and she gave him a sleepy smile. He plucked her from the vine that he found growing out of her belly like a green umbilical cord, wrapped her in a bathrobe, and wheeled her into the house where he had prepared a nice, warm bath. After he had finished cleaning her, Nico dried her skin and dressed her in a silk blouse with a low decolletage to show off her taut bosom. He slipped on a pair of lace panties and helped her into a flowy linen skirt. The woman never once fought him or fussed. He liked this very much. He was careful not to speak to her – if she didn't learn to talk, she couldn't talk back. Women, he thought, were much more attractive when they kept their mouths shut, and the longer she went without speaking, the more used to staying silent she would become.

  Once dressed, he helped her to her feet. He walked with her to the door. He realized she was mimicking his gait, and he hated it; she was strutting like a man. So, he pranced about and wagged his hips as if to say, *"*Like this! This is how a *woman* walks!*"* She caught on quickly. He wiped his brow. That was a close call.

Nico took her to the kitchen. He had never been much of a cook. What was the point? He had figured one day he would marry, and it would be his wife's job to fuss over the meals. Nico showed her where all the cooking accessories were and piled a stack of cookbooks on the counter. He hoped it was everything she'd need. If it wasn't, she'd have to ask his mother for advice or figure it out for herself, borrow something from the neighbors, or request an allowance to go to the store.

Then Nico took her to the living room. He wiped a finger across a coffee table and frowned at the dust he picked up. They walked over to the utility closet where he demonstrated all of the cleaning supplies: mops and brooms and polishers, scouring agents, and more. He silently instructed her on the washing machine and clothes dryer, and he showed her how to set up the ironing board.

Finally, Nico pulled out a map, pointed to the grocery store, and handed her a shopping list. Next to the back door was a rack full of clothes that needed dry cleaning, and the garbage needed taking out. The more he showed her, the more ideas he came up with. The possibilities for women's work, he felt, were endless.

The brand-new woman's shoulders sagged, and her eyelids drooped. Nico sensed she was overwhelmed and, honestly, he was also getting tired. He supposed it was time for them to retire to the bedroom where he could show her *the most important thing of all*.

In his room, Nico dimmed the lights and approached the woman hungrily. He began to kiss her neck and shoulders. He tossed her shirt to the wayside and unzipped her skirt, flinging it to the floor. He went to remove her panties when he spotted a dark red liquid dripping down between her legs. The sight made him gasp and gag. Nico grabbed her hand and dragged her to the bathroom, pointed down at her in disgust with one hand while shielding his eyes with the other, and motioned to the cabinet under the sink where there was a bucket, soap, and a rag. He noted the tears in her eyes as he slammed the door and thought, *Good, she should be ashamed*.

Nico took a seat on the edge of his bed and stewed angrily. His mother should have prepared him for this. He knew it had something to do with making a baby, and his mother desperately wanted grandchildren, but there had to be something to prevent that disgusting mess.

Rubbing his eyes, Nico lay down, exhausted. Maybe if the woman cleaned up – really deeply sanitized – they could still have sex.

But nothing more between them happened that night because Nico fell into a deep, dreamless sleep.

2

The phone next to the bed rang incessantly. When Nico opened his eyes, he saw the room was flooded with daylight and realized he had overslept. He grabbed the phone and muttered a groggy, "Hello?"

"How did everything turn out yesterday?"

It was his mother.

"Fine," he said. He glanced around the room – no sign of the woman, but the bathroom door was open a crack. "She was ready to harvest, just like you said she would be."

"Excellent," his mother said. "I can't wait to meet her. Bring her over for dinner. I'm making a roast."

She hung up and Nico got to his feet. He cautiously walked to the bathroom, peeked inside, and was relieved to find it spotless. As he headed out of his room and descended the stairs looking for his new wife, he was struck by a pungent smell. He couldn't quite place it until he stood in the doorway to the kitchen.

He found her hunched over the counter, covered from head to toe in bleached white flour, packing a crust into a pie tin. She looked up and gave Nico a wink. The kitchen was a disaster, but he now knew what he'd smelled. On the counter behind her were several pies, all fresh out of the oven. They bubbled over with a dark liquid and steamed with the aroma of caramelized sugar.

Nico walked over and stuck his finger into one of them, gave it a lick, and sighed. Cherry? Or mixed berry? Either way, the pie filling was scrumptious. His mother would certainly be impressed.

Nico beamed at the woman, forgetting all about the bathroom. He wanted to tell her she was brilliant, the best wife he ever could have picked. But he dared not speak to her (*especially not with praise as his first words to her – why ruin things so soon?*), so he simply grabbed her and gave her a deep, passionate kiss. When he let go, she stared at up him with a look of confusion. No matter, he thought. She'd get used to his affection sooner or later. And if she didn't – well that was her problem, not his.

Nico checked the clock and realized he'd slept half the day away, but there was still plenty of time before dinner. He decided to go out for a run. When he returned from exercising, he showered. By the time he was dressed and ready, five pies were cooling, and the kitchen was clean.

They gathered the pies and headed to his mother's. On the way over, he realized it was inevitable that the woman would learn to speak. He decided he would go ahead and lay down some ground rules.

"Now listen, you're going to meet my family," he explained, "and there are a few things you should know. Do not tell them where you come from. Before you speak, look at me. I'll nod if it's okay for you to answer. If it isn't, I'll answer for you. In general, you should never speak unless spoken to."

The woman gazed out the window as she listened.

"Do you understand?" Nico asked, looking for confirmation.

She finally turned to him and gave him a petite smile, the kind a child gives to a small animal when they pet it for the first time.

"My family has very progressive feelings about womanhood," he continued, "but I do not. And because I gave you life, I made you, you must obey me. Got it?"

She kept smiling and gave him a small nod. Nico wondered how much she understood. It didn't matter, he supposed. She was just a woman. Didn't matter if she understood anything at all. She just needed to obey.

"You've done very well so far. Just keep doing it. Do what I tell you, and everything will be just fine."

He asked himself why he hadn't planted some woman seeds years ago; it was the smartest thing he'd ever done.

3

When they arrived at his mother's, Nico proudly introduced his wife. His mother kept trying to engage her in small talk, but each time Nico interrupted, never letting her speak. Just because his mother gave him the seeds, it didn't mean that the woman was hers, after all. *He'd* done the watering and fertilizing. *He'd* pruned her leaves and picked off the bugs. She was *his* wife, not his mother's. He wasn't going to let her assert control.

"Pray tell, dear, what is your name?" asked his mother as she passed the woman a bowl of scalloped potatoes.

Nico crossed his arms over his chest like a petulant child. "That is my decision, not hers." He shoveled a piece of roast into his mouth and smacked as he chewed.

"Rhea," said the woman to his mother.

Nico's mouth fell open and a half-masticated piece of beef fell out. That *bitch*. She'd taken advantage of him while he was eating. Rage boiled like acid in his stomach. He'd make her pay for her insolence when they got home.

His mother put her hand over the woman's. "What a beautiful name," she said. Then she turned to Nico. "You're sure to make a handsome family together in due time."

"I know you want grandchildren, Mother," he spat in thinly veiled disdain. "But we will provide them when *I'm* ready and not a moment sooner."

His mother and his wife just wanly smiled.

After dinner, his mother placed a pie on the table.

"No, thank you, Mother. I'm full," Nico tried to protest.

His mother ignored him and cut a giant slice. She slapped it onto his plate. Somehow it was still hot and steaming. As soon as the smell hit Nico's nose, he inexplicably found himself hungry again. His mother stood next to the table in silence and watched as he began shoveling it into his maw.

He thought it was so delicious that he couldn't stop eating, even helped himself to seconds, then thirds. His wife and mother sat in silence as he single-handedly finished off one of the pies. Sticky red filling fell off his fork, and syrupy juices dripped down his chin as he gobbled up bite after bite. Eventually, Nico finished off pie number two, groaning in pleasure as the berry filling exploded on his taste buds.

He started in on pie number three as he glared at his new wife. *Rhea.* What a ridiculous name. But at least the woman could cook. And he would make sure she learned to never talk back.

4

On their way home that evening, Nico's gut gurgled with indigestion. He had meant to admonish Rhea all the way home and, upon arrival, demonstrate his authority. A few bruises would serve as a reminder never to disobey him again. But his stomach kept flopping and roiling. He pulled into the driveway and parked but struggled to get out of the car.

Why did I eat so much pie? he thought regretfully. *I should have taken it more slowly and exercised restraint.*

"I need air!" Nico gasped. Rhea exited the car and went around to the driver's side. She helped him out of the car, led him into the garden, and sat down next to him on a bench. He moaned and clutched at his abdomen. The world began to spin. He broke out in a cold sweat and turned a sickly yellow.

Rhea's punishment would just have to wait.

"I need to go inside and lie down!" he belched, but as soon as he stood, he knew he wouldn't make it that far.

Nico stood and stumbled into the vegetable patch, grabbing a bean pole to try and maintain his balance. His diaphragm spasmed violently, and he began to projectile vomit. Dark red globs of pie flew across the garden, magenta juices streamed out of his mouth. Nico retched, and red liquid dribbled down his chin. He heaved again, and cherry-colored chunks flew out his nose, and the third time, he gagged until a sea of tiny, mucous-covered seeds and berries thickly carpeted the ground.

When he finally finished vomiting, Nico lost consciousness and collapsed.

Rhea walked over to him and observed his still body. His breathing grew more and more shallow until, finally, Nico sighed his last breath.

Rhea went to the middle of the garden and swept the seeds he had vomited out of the way until there was a bare patch of earth the same length as Nico's body. She dug a hole with her hands. She worked late into the night, diligently excavating the dirt until, sometime just before dawn, she had a grave large enough for Nico's corpse. She rolled him into the ground and covered him with the seeds and moist soil.

Looking about, she spotted the hose coiled against the outside of the house. She fetched it and watered everything down.

5

A few months later just above Nico's grave, the seeds had grown into a garden full of baby girls with jet black hair and freckled skin. One by one, the girls opened their eyes – they were a brilliant blue that sparkled just like their father's. The babies lay naked among the cabbage leaves, babbling and cooing, finally ready for harvest. Nico's mother showed up right on time.

The second the old crone entered the garden and saw the babies, she began gleefully laughing. She ran over and embraced Rhea.

"Oh, thank you, thank you," she said with a tear in her eye.

Rhea laughed as she hugged her mother-in-law in return.

"Don't be silly," Rhea said over her shoulder. "It was you that brought them to life."

The old woman leaned back and gazed out over the garden full of grandchildren, wistfully thinking back on the last few years. She had hoped her son would turn out differently. She had hoped he might be humbled, learn and grow. But, alas, some gardens were beyond weeding, had to be razed, reimagined, and started again. It was a shame his own beliefs and actions had led to his demise, but what a magical new beginning had sprouted in his place.

She walked over and plucked up one of the babies, tickled its belly, and kissed its cheeks. It gurgled and showered her with its tinkly little laughter, the future burning brightly behind its eyes, proof that the old ways still worked.

Help is on the Way- Cat Voleur

The knife pushes in further when I try to stand. There's no clear way for me to get to my feet without leaning forward onto it.

The damn thing has to come out. Now.

I refuse, *refuse*, to die before the police get here. Help is on the way. I just have to survive long enough for it to reach me.

It's a waiting game.

I look around for something that will staunch the bleeding once I've gotten the weapon out. I notice the fuzzy pink bathmat first, which is already within reach, but that hardly seems sanitary. Scanning over the drawers under the sink and the medicine cabinet, I wonder if there's a first aid kit in here somewhere. There might be, but I'd need one with gauze. Jumbo band-aids aren't going to cut it for this, and there's not going to be a lot of time to dig around.

My eyes land on the towel.

I am sitting with my back braced against the bathroom door. The towel rack is opposite me. Even with me being lightheaded it won't take more than twenty seconds at most to stand up, grab it, and sit back down with it pressed against the wound.

But the knife has to come out first, which is where the risk comes.

I'm sure the blade is bad for the baby.

The thought comes out of nowhere and it's so ridiculous that I don't know if I should laugh or cry.

Not even an hour has passed since I shared the news. Part of me still doesn't understand where it all went so wrong. Part of me can't accept.

As I sat down to dinner with the man I loved, nothing could have prepared me for the morbid mathematics I'm now trying to run through in my mind.

Can I spare the blood?

How long until they arrive?

Will I survive just sitting?

Surely they'll be here any minute, but I don't know if Donnie is dead. I don't know if I'm alone, if there will be an altercation, if shots will be fired. If I have to get down on the ground, I won't be able to like this. I'm steadily losing blood, and I'm not mobile with this damn thing stuck in me.

And the blade is bad for the baby.

The room is unsteady, and I force myself to look at the towel until things stop spinning.

Before I can go for it, I press my head back against the door to see if I can hear him.

I can't.

It feels like a long time since the banging from the other side subsided, but I listen anyway. I'm sure his breathing must be as ragged as my own, if he is breathing at all.

I know I got him pretty bad.

We have been together nearly eight years, since even before high school. I've known him nearly my whole life. How is it possible that he was such a stranger to me the entire time? How could I not have known?

I cannot count on him being dead, but I can count on him being weakened. The lock may be flimsy, the door itself may be flimsy without my weight behind it, but I got him *good*. There is no way he has the strength to break through in the time it will take me to grab the towel and sit back down.

Twenty seconds. At most.

I brace myself and get my hand on the handle of the weapon.

It hurts more than I thought possible, and takes more strength than I fear I have.

But with a sharp yank, somehow, mercifully, the knife is out.

I'm up. Shakily, but I'm up.

The towel catches my fall as I grab for it. No sooner have I let out a gasp of pain than I hear the doorknob begin to rattle behind me. The warmth is leaking from my body as I turn back to look.

There is so much blood.

The bathroom is full of it.

It pools under where I was sitting.

It drips down the yellow door where my head was resting. It is splattered against the side of the sickly green tub and takes the shape of my foot where I stepped on the bathmat.

The room spins again.

The doorknob rattles.

I tear the towel free as I slide back to the ground. This time I face the door, bracing it with my legs, not having enough time to consider if this position is as good.

It feels sturdier, but it requires more of my fleeting strength than I have to give.

I roll the towel up clumsily and press it to the gash in my abdomen. This time it feels more like a bruise than a sharp pain, and I wonder if it means I'm dying that I can't feel the ache as deep anymore.

I wonder if something else in me has died, but cannot allow my brain to form the thought fully. It is too terrible.

On top of everything it's just too terrible.

As I struggle to keep my vision focused, I see horrors in the red stains. The way his hand swings to strike my cheek, the flash of his anger as he yanks the hair out of my scalp, the distorted face of a stranger as the blade slides in.

I was so excited to tell him.

I had no delusions that he would be as happy as I was, but I could not have ever predicted that he would be capable of such violence. Not only was he capable, but there was virtually no hesitation between my words and the first strike.

At worst I had thought there would be an uncomfortable conversation about the thing that had recently been made illegal here, about maybe driving out of state. Not this. Never this.

The second he knew, I was already dead to him.

It's getting harder to keep my eyes open and my head up, and the terrible memories at bay. For a while, I don't think I succeed.

"Hannah," his voice croaks from the other side of the door.

My blood freezes as my vision snaps back into focus.

"Shut up."

"Hannah…"

"No." I don't know how long I was out for, but it could not have been too long. I don't like how much stronger his voice sounds than mine.

"Open the door…"

"No!"

"Hannah… I was just trying to stop you."

"To stop me?" I sob, incredulous. *I* had been trying to stop *him*. I had been acting in self-defense. I had just wanted to have a nice dinner with my fiancé, to tell him the good news. "To stop me from what?"

"From hurting the baby…"

I don't have time to ask what he means before the door bursts open.

I am too startled to even scream, but the fear and confusion quickly dissipate when I see the officers standing over me.

"Oh, thank god." I made it. I survived. The nightmare is over.

A man in uniform pulls me up to my feet and I let him take most of my weight as I continue crying. "I'm so glad you're here. He just started attacking me and…and…"

I falter as my wrists are brought behind my back.

His words sink in.

From hurting the baby.

I think about what the scene must look like to the officers. The distraught man pleading with me to stop, to open the door, the bathroom filled with blood, the knife covered in my own fingerprints.

But I'm the one who called them mid-scuffle.

I'm the one who was stabbed.

They have to know that I'm the victim in all this.

Don't they?

The metal around my wrists before I'm even in the ambulance, while I'm still bleeding, while my baby is still in danger… it makes me doubt.

Everything.

I doubt everything.

Bedrest- Yvonne Dutchover

The ceiling fan hitched at the same point in its rotation, at about two o'clock. *Dun-dun ... dun-dun ... dun-dun.* The rhythm mirrored the throbbing in Sara's head. Her eyes pulsed in time with the fan, and the sound of her heartbeat filled her ears. Her eyes lost focus as she followed the fan's blades.

Her world had shrunk to this room, these four walls with their sloped ceiling, and the childhood bed she rested on like a magic carpet ride to nowhere. She dozed in and out of a dream about the lake, floating on her back in the cold, deep water and watching a blue sky so bright it hurt her eyes.

She is at the old flooded quarry again, following her younger sister Ana up the chalky cliff. Sara is ten years older, but her feet drag with dread. Eleven-year-old Ana glances over her knobby shoulder as she scrambles up the granite like a mountain goat. She smiles and gestures impatiently. *Hurry up!* Ana climbs to the tallest ledge of the cliff. Sara joins her, panting. Thirty, forty feet stretch between them and the indigo water below.

A nervous-looking girl about Ana's age stands at the edge next to them, along with a sunburned boy who looks like her older brother. The boy dares the girl, and then she is flying, her arms and legs pinwheeling. He follows, holding his body as straight as an arrow. Screams and laughter carry from down below, and then the loud smack of their bodies hitting the water.

Anxiety tightens Sara's stomach. Why is she so afraid? Why is it so hard for her to jump when everyone else does it easily? The cliff at the cove is a rite of passage in this small town. But Sara hates the sensation of her stomach plunging as she free-falls into open space, and she's never jumped from this high before. At least nine people have drowned at Crystal Cove. One teenager broke his neck when he hit the water. Like many flooded quarries, the depths hide dangers you can't see from the surface.

Dun-dun ... dun-dun. Her pounding heart reverberated in her ears and woke her up, for good this time.

Where was she?

Sara wasn't at the old flooded quarry; she was in her old bedroom at her mother's house. And she wasn't twenty-one anymore. Sara caressed her stomach protectively. She was a thirty-one-year-old woman expecting her first baby. *"Little fish, big fish, swimming in the water,"* Sara sang to herself hoarsely. She hadn't spoken to anyone yet today.

She found herself singing old songs she barely remembered, quoting lines from books or the radio. With no one to talk to, her mind snagged on certain phrases and repeated them like a tea kettle letting off steam. "I lost my heart, under the bridge to that little girl, so much to me," Sara sang.

One way or another, she needed help. She spoke to only Christina and Ashley. She desperately wanted her mother or Dr. Akin. Surely even he would help her now. Sara had come back to her mother's house ten days ago.

"Mija, your blood pressure is too high. If we don't get it down, this could develop into preeclampsia." Her mother, Catarina Hernandez, had been a physician's assistant for a busy OB-GYN practice in Chicago. So long ago it seemed like another lifetime.

The air in the third-floor bedroom felt as thick, hot, and sticky as oatmeal on this late August morning. The fan did little

more than push warm air across her face. The electrical grid
was often strained, especially in summer, and they had all been asked to conserve. People used to ignore the alerts, but after a few incidents when the rolling "temporary" blackouts had lasted for days, everyone listened when asked to conserve now.

    Had it really been ten days?

    At least she still had her notebook. Sara pulled it out from her hiding place between the mattress and the boxspring. She turned to the page where she made a small pencil mark each morning. Ten marks. Today was August 22. Her due date was September 17.

    A premie's risk of medical complications was lower the closer the baby was to full term. Her mother's goal was for Sara to reach her 36th week of pregnancy. Sara had made it. In fact, in only five days, she would be at 37 weeks.

    Sara had come to her mother ten days ago because she was worried. The doctor at the Army base had delivered hundreds, if not thousands, of babies. But Dr. Akin had been pulled out of retirement and dozed frequently.

    He nodded as Sara talked, but he was almost completely deaf and she couldn't tell if he was listening. "We'll see how you're doing on your next visit," he'd told her, and then patted her on the back as though she were a petulant child instead of a woman who had been tracking a long list of physical symptoms.

Her mother had been a different story. She'd studied Sara's swollen feet and hands, then taken her blood pressure. After her examination, she squeezed Sara's hands in hers, staring at her seriously with her piercing hazel eyes. Her mother didn't overreact, so if she was concerned, there was reason to be.

"I can't give you blood pressure medication because it's a blood thinner. That's dangerous if you end up needing a C-section, and you might need one if we have to deliver this baby early. So the best thing we can do right now is to try to control your blood pressure by limiting your activity as much as possible. You can stay in your old room. With the water closet up there, you won't have to walk far for the bathroom."

"What about the library?" The thought of leaving the books and the treasures in the storage room unnerved her more than she would have guessed.

"I wouldn't ask you to leave unless I thought it was the best thing for you. I'll call them. Don't worry. I'll bring your books," her mother had said. "Is there some way to get in touch with Matthew?"

"I'll leave word at the base in case he calls," Sara said.

Matthew had been deployed recently. Sara assumed that meant they were sending him to the front because he couldn't say where they were sending him, and he wasn't sure how reliable the mail would be.

On that first evening, Sara had napped on the couch while her mother had driven to Sara and Matthew's apartment. She returned with clothes, toiletries, and books. They ate dinner around seven, then her mother cleared the table. Sara started to stand.

"No, no," her mother waved her away. "After tonight, I don't want you leaving your bed except for the bathroom." Then her mother's shoulders slumped.

"What's wrong?" Sara asked.

"Charles called before dinner. I need to check on your sister. She's starting to spot." "No," Sara whispered. "Not again."

Sara was about five weeks from her due date, and Ana was about three months behind her. They were all excited that the cousins would be so close in age. Unlike Sara and Ana who were ten years apart.

"Women spot for all kinds of reasons." But her mother didn't look at Sara. She focused on scrubbing the plates in front of her. "Listen, sometimes people stop by my office. They might ask for me."

"Who?" Sara asked.

"Women who need help. I don't know much more than that. I rarely do. And it's better if you don't either," her mother said wryly. She put the last plate on the drying rack and left the kitchen. Sara heard her rifling through things in her office. Her mother returned with a backpack. "If someone stops by, this is what she's looking for."

"What's inside?"

"Supplies." Her mother frowned, staring at Sara as though she were examining her. Then she nodded as though she'd come to a decision. She opened the bag and pulled out a book. Sara read the title, *The Old Farmers' Almanac* . Her mother opened it to a page marked with a sealed envelope.

"This is where she should go." Her mother tapped the address printed on the envelope. The edge in her mother's voice made the hair on Sara's arms rise. Sara didn't know what this was, but it felt dangerous.

"What's going on?"

Her mother smiled sadly. "Helping women who need it." She kissed the top of Sara's head. "Go to bed, mija. We need to get that blood pressure down."

Sara stared at the open almanac. She couldn't make out the address from this angle, but she saw that the page was open to a moon phase calendar. Her mother had taught her how to track her menstrual cycle and ovulation with the moon long ago. They'd gone back to the old ways after abortion and then birth control were outlawed. Sara wouldn't be surprised if her mother helped her patients learn these methods too.

As a physician's assistant, her mother turned no one away. She always had boxes of food, supplies, and clothes in all sizes. She said it was for her patients who were struggling, but Sara had always known, deep down. It had been easier to pretend not to. Her mother helped women who were pregnant. And she helped women who didn't want to be pregnant. And she helped women who wanted to run.

Sara had tried and failed to sleep while her mother was gone. When she returned, hours later, Sara was still awake and waiting for her on the couch. "How's Ana?" she asked.

Her mother's face looked drawn and tired, but she smiled and held up both thumbs. "She's doing okay. I'll check on her again tomorrow."

It was late, and they said goodnight.

On the second morning, her mother brought her breakfast in bed. Then she left to check on her patients and Ana. Sara looked through the box of books her mother had brought for her. She read most of that second day. Her mother hadn't returned home by six, so Sara made herself dinner, despite her mother's admonition to stay in bed. Her mother had many patients, and Sara didn't know when she would return.

On the third morning, Christina and Ashley had come with breakfast.

"Catarina has an emergency delivery. She's been there all night," Christina said. "Is it Ana?" Sara asked.

The two sisters exchanged a look. "Charles didn't tell us which patient it was," Christina said quickly.

The sisters were two of the most active volunteers in Charles' church and with the local government, although that was mostly the same thing. They always showed up during an illness or emergency, but intimidating with their efficiency, organization, and connections to power.

Men made the laws, but they relied on women to enforce them.

"We'll stay with you until your mother is free," Ashley said.

"Your precious baby is the most important thing right now," Christina added.

Sara shook her head, feeling dizzy. It was hard to tell who was speaking. Their voices sounded so similar, and each started one sentence before the other had stopped talking. The two women were a few years younger than Sara, but they had a brood of children between them.

Ashley and Christina had been born less than a year apart. They looked enough alike to be twins, except Ashley had hair almost to her waist, and Christina had cut her hair extremely short. "I don't have enough time to bother with all that," she explained.

On the fourth morning, the door creaked open. Sara was dozing when they brought her breakfast. The sisters stood there for several seconds before she registered that they were there. Ashley set a tray of food down on the bedside table.

The sisters pulled extra pillows from the bed and dropped them onto the floor. "Dear Lord," Christina began, "please shine your healing light onto this woman, this vessel protecting a sacred soul. Please bless us with this child …"

She droned on and on. Sara closed her eyes. The room was warm and stuffy. Both women had a faintly sweet smell, like a scent that remains in a bottle after the perfume has evaporated.

The fan swirled the stale air around the room. Sara's temples throbbed in beat with her pulse. There was a pause in the litany, and Sara opened her eyes, barely. Slits of light entered her vision and she noticed the corner of one of her library books sneaking out from under the covers.

Dun-dun-dun-dun-dun-dun. The tempo in her temples sped up. Oh shit. She'd forgotten to hide the damn book. But she hadn't expected them so early. She closed her eyes again, praying that Christina hadn't seen it. Sara slid the lemon-yellow coverlet over the book as nonchalantly as she could manage.

But Christina had seen. She pulled the book out, and her lips had thinned into a grim, straight line as she read the title. Sara fought the urge to snatch the book back.

"You shouldn't be reading this," Christina said disapprovingly.

Sara decided to play dumb. "I found an old box of books up here. I was passing the time." She thought about saying it was one of her old books from college, but thought that might make her situation worse.

Christina's eyes searched the room and found the box. Sara's heart beat faster. Christina opened the cardboard flaps, then she flipped through the various paperbacks and hardcovers.

"All of these books are on the list. You should be resting. Not filling your mind with this filth."

"I have nothing else to do," Sara said.

Christina took the box and slipped it under her arm,

"Please, I haven't seen a magazine or newspaper in weeks. The internet is always down." Christina left without another word. Ashley pursed her lips, but her eyes still looked kind.

That was the difference between Christina and Ashley. Ashley worried about following the rules, but the rules didn't make her forget you were a person. And a neighbor.

Sara texted and called her mother, but there had been no answer. She should have left then, Sara knew now. But she hadn't realized how much trouble she was in, and her strength had faded dramatically since only a few days ago.

Sometime early on the fifth morning, the sisters had taken Sara's phone and purse before she woke. And then, well, she wasn't sure. The days blended together, and it was hard to know what had happened when. Over the next few days, she raged, complained, demanded answers, and begged for information about her mother or Ana. But no matter what she did, the sisters said nothing.

Ten days.

Ten days since she had agreed to come here.

Eight days since she'd last seen her mother.

Fifteen days since she'd had word about Matthew.

Sara sat up and rested her back against the headboard of the white full-sized bed, elevating her swollen feet on two pillows. Her temple pulsed with each heartbeat, heat flushed her face, and her toes and the roots of her hair tingled. She rested her notebook on her expanding belly and closed her eyes. She had started to collect quotes from book and song lyrics for her daughter in her notebook a few months ago.

Was her baby okay? Sara opened her eyes and focused on her stomach. Something wasn't right. She had never been so aware of her eyes as spheres before. The pressure behind them was palpable.

"Oil is up forty dollars a barrel as conflicts in Texas and Louisiana have disrupted production and distribution," a voice intoned from the radio downstairs.

"The president will be on soon," one of the sisters said

The president had started the daily updates at the beginning of his third term. The briefing and prayer combo were broadcast at noon, a one-two punch that lulled Sara into sleep. She didn't understand why she was so tired when all she did was lie around all day. But after meals, she could barely keep her eyes open and usually napped for several hours until the voices woke her for the next one.

Her only lifelines right now, without her mother, sister, or husband, were the two sisters downstairs. And the radio they listened to incessantly. Radios, unlike TVs, could run off batteries instead of electricity.

"Who called earlier?"

"Charles."

Sara listened intently. Charles was her brother-in-law, and the pastor of the largest church in town. If Charles was calling, then at least someone in her family was keeping tabs on her. Sara hadn't been completely abandoned.

"I hope you told him we have everything under control."

That sounded like Christina. She was the bossier sister and always worried about appearances, what people thought. Sara's bedroom was the only room on the third floor of their house, formerly an attic with a sloped ceiling and dormer windows. It had been a nursery once. A narrow staircase led from the kitchen to the room, presumably for the servants or slaves, if the old history books were reliable. Sound carried up here easily from the kitchen. "Thats not why he called; What did he want?"

Ashley spoke hesitantly. "He said to keep her stable until tomorrow. He'll adopt the baby."

"Smart. Really the best thing for everyone," Christina said approvingly. "Poor Ana," Ashley said. "She's such a sweetheart."

Wait. Had they said *adopt*? Were they talking about Sara? That made no sense. Ana was having a baby of her own. Why would Charles adopt her baby? Sara clutched her belly. She would never agree to it. Neither would Matthew. They couldn't make her. There were no laws that permitted it. Unless the books maybe? No. She was being paranoid, imagining a conspiracy.

The room throbbed each time Sara's heartbeat, the walls pulsating like a second heart keeping time with her own. And now that double heartbeat faster and faster, filling her with panic. Sara struggled up to her elbows and swung her legs over the side of the bed. She had to get out. But her head swam with dizziness, and the room spun around her. She took a deep breath. She wasn't sure she could stand, let alone walk.

The baby kicked, but Sara barely felt it, a small flutter. Lately, the baby's movements felt weak and far away. Was the baby even a she? Sara didn't know, but she had begun thinking of the little being growing inside as *her.* And she belonged to Sara. No one would take her away.

But the movements had become so faint. Sara needed medical help. She needed information. She needed to find a way out of this room.

"It's your turn," one of the sisters said.

"I went last time," the other complained.

Was that Christina or Ashley? The sister's voices were so similar it was hard to tell, and Sara couldn't remember who had brought her last meal. When the sisters talked to her in person, they used a sweet, cajoling tone. But when they were alone in the kitchen, their voices sounded low, conspiratorial, like they belonged to different women. Sara shivered, despite the heat.

The bickering continued until someone finally huffed, "All right."

"Don't forget the milk."

The risers creaked as slow, steady footsteps ascended. Sara leaned forward and a wave of dizziness rushed through her. She shook her head, trying to focus. She hid the notebook between the mattress and the boxspring. Finally, after what felt like minutes, someone fumbled with the locked bedroom door. Ashley made her way into the room deliberately and set a tray down on the bedside table. Today her blond hair was in a bun, and she wore a white dress with a full skirt that looked like something you'd wear to a party instead of taking care of a bedridden woman.

"Why are you sitting up? You're all flushed," Ashley said.

Ashley might take pity on her. Christina would not. The sisters were her only tether to the outside world, and Sara needed them as allies. Or, at least, not as enemies. She sat up straighter and tried to clear her head.

Sara glanced at her lunch. On the tray, an apple, a peanut butter and jelly sandwich on homemade bread, and milk. Ashley plumped up the pillows behind her, and Sara rested against them. Ashley handed her the glass of thick, creamy milk. Sara forced down a sip, choking a little. Better to get it over with. Both sisters would stare at her until she drained it. Sara loathed the taste of milk. It gave her terrible gas and stomach cramps, but no matter what she said, the sisters brought it to her with every meal. "I'm lactose intolerant," Sarah had told them.

"Nonsense, milk is good for mothers."

Sara wouldn't complain about the milk today. She swallowed another sip grimly, and Ashley nodded approvingly.

The two sisters had inherited a dairy farm, and they had plenty of milk to go around. That could not be said of everything. Some items were out of stock at times. They might return to shelves or they might not, and the radio did not explain why. Pork was sporadic. Peanut butter was rare, and Sara was happy to have some. Jellies and jams were canned in town and almost always available, although she didn't care for all of the flavors. Beef and chicken were staples around here. People who produced their own food were in control of their supply chain.

"Have you heard from my mother?"

"I told you. Your mother has been delayed. Drink your milk."

Sara swallowed again, grimacing. Almost half the glass was gone. To cover the thick taste, she bit the apple, avoiding the bruise on the skin. It was one of the first of the season. Most of the apples would be harvested next month, in September, and this early batch was small and starchy. She chewed slowly to avoid drinking more milk.

Sara decided she would act pathetic this time. Not that it was much of a stretch.

"Something's wrong. Look at how swollen I am." Sara held up her left hand. Her normally slender fingers were fat little sausages. "And my feet don't fit in any of my shoes. All I can wear are slippers." It wasn't only her hands and her feet, either. Everything on her was swollen—her lips, eyelids, even her earlobes were puffy.

"That's why you're on bedrest, silly," Ashley averted her eyes.

She would try another tactic. "Have you heard from Matthew?" Sara's voice cracked on her husband's name.

"Now don't you go worrying yourself. Matthew is doing God's work, and so are you. You need to keep yourself strong and healthy for this baby."

"Has he called or written?"

Ashley's eyes softened. "Not here. But if you give me a name, I'll call the base and ask if they have any news."

The church bell began to toll. *One,* a long pause. *Two.* Two bells repeated meant guilty.

What if her mother had been caught doing something she shouldn't? Maybe that's why she hadn't come. The pressure built inside Sara's head. She didn't know how much longer she could stand it. Sara held her breath, but the slow tolling continued until it reached twelve. She breathed deeply. Only the noontime bell.

Sara told Ashley the phone number for the base's main line, and Ashley repeated it a few times until they both felt confident she would remember it. Ashley turned toward the door.

"No, please. Don't leave me." Sara begged, naked need in her voice. "I don't know what's happening. My mother told me my blood pressure was too high, but she and Ana haven't come to see me in days. I barely feel the baby moving. And I'm worried about my sister. Mom said she was starting to spot the last time we talked."

"Your sister has had some complications. But it's not my place to talk about them, and you're getting all worked up." Ashley looked at her kindly, but she glanced at the door, clearly ready to leave. The daily presidential remarks were the highlight of her day. When she spoke about the president, she sounded like a fan of one of those old-fashioned rock stars Sara had read about in the forgotten magazines in the library. Was anyone making music anymore? Writing books? Surely somewhere.

"I'm not supposed to tell you this, but your sister is coming to sit with you tonight," Ashley confided.

"Ana's coming?" Relief flooded her voice.

Ashley nodded. "But don't ask her too many questions."

"Why?"

"It's better that way."

"What about my mother?"

Ashley paused at the door. Her eyes darted around the room, not meeting Sara's. She cleared her throat. "I don't know where she is right now," she said.

That seemed like a careful evasion. *Right now.* Sara started to ask another question, but how to say it eluded her. Lately, she felt like someone who'd had a stroke. Sara knew what she wanted to say, but it took longer for her to remember the right combination of words.

"I'll leave you to your lunch. Make sure you drink the milk." Ashley closed the door behind her.

Locked in. Again. The sisters wouldn't return until dinner and prayers.

"Dammit!" Sara hit the mattress with her fist and barely felt the pressure on her swollen skin. She searched between the mattress and boxspring. When her fingers found nothing, panic made the heat rush to her head and feet again.

Finally, her fingers grasped the small notebook. She pulled it out with swollen, clumsy fingers. She kept track with a mark each morning. Now she doubted herself. Had she forgotten earlier? Had she missed a day? She squeezed her temples. The nonstop pressure made it hard to focus. She didn't think she'd made a mistake, which definitely meant today was ten.

Ten days since her mother convinced her to stay.

It was the second time she'd returned to this room. Catarina had been recruited to this small town when Sara was sixteen, a junior in high school, and Ana was starting kindergarten. Medical staff were in short supply. Ana had been absorbed into this community in a way that neither Catarina nor Sara ever had. Maybe it was because Ana had grown up here. Of course, her marriage to Charles, a town and church leader, had helped. Sara had lived here until high school graduation, then left for college, planning to never return.

She'd come back the first time during the spring semester of her junior year. Everyone thought it was temporary. Many colleges planned to shut down for a few weeks to contain the viruses spreading among the dorms and cafeterias. Sara had unpacking in this attic room then, unaware she would never return to her university, never officially graduate. She had attended college for almost three years before the laws had begun to change. Now there was even talk of prohibiting high school for girls. At least she'd had those years of freedom. Ana never had.

Sara started working in the town library when she was twenty-one, after it became obvious she wouldn't return to college anytime

soon. She shelved books, read during the
children's story hour. She still worked there ten years later, although now her duties were a little different.

Every month, more people visited the library to research topics like edible plants, canning vegetables, and basic first aid. The information online wasn't reliable anymore. All those words floating like poisonous spores looking for a hospitable place to grow and spread. Disinformation, they called it. Some seemed like coordinated cyberattacks by hostile governments or hackers.

Some seemed like pranks. Others seemed designed to hurt or even kill people. To what end, no one knew or would admit.

She'd rummaged around in storage and found the old wooden card catalogs, and she had even managed to scrounge up an old typewriter that still worked in a secondhand store. She'd started creating cards for all of the books that had come in since the card catalogs had been retired. That task alone was enough to keep any librarian busy for years.

Sara used an old two-drawer filing cabinet as her desk, and she always came up with a stack of new index cards for the card catalog. In between typing sessions, she explored the storage room. She found books and magazines and CDs and cassettes and DVDs and VHS tapes.

There was no rhyme or reason to how these materials were organized. Books were mixed with music and magazines, everything shoved into boxes.

No one asked about them; no one came for them. They were forgotten boxes filled with confiscated media. Had they ended up stored in their small-town library because they were on the way to the army base? Were they the library's old materials? Sara was afraid to ask, afraid someone would take them away if she said something. She was careful. She took only one item at a time, ready to hide it at any moment if someone came looking for her. No one ever did. Over time, Sara grew bolder. She started taking a book or magazine home with her each night. First, to her mother's, and later to her husband's.

Her husband wasn't around much. Matthew was often deployed, and when he was home, he was so tired and shell-shocked, he let her do as she liked. She was twenty-nine when she became his bride. Ancient by town standards. Ana had told her it was time. Sara didn't have to marry Matthew, but she sensed that this time was a suggestion. In the future, it would become a command.

She could not have stayed single for much longer. People were already gossiping about her. Sara wasn't sure that she was gay, but she had dated a few girls in college. Somehow, rumors of that had followed her home.

Matthew was twenty-four, and he followed her lead in most things. She could have chosen worse. She read, and Matthew didn't ask what she was reading. He didn't ask about the different books or magazines or sometimes music she brought home each night. And she almost grew to love him for that. In a place that monitored how she dressed, behaved, and spoke, to be left alone with her thoughts was an unexpected gift. She started carrying a little notebook, small enough to fit in her pocket. She touched her stomach. She hoped her baby was okay. She was writing down these quotes from books and lyrics from songs for her daughter. One day, she would give the notebook to her. Messages from an abandoned world.

> "To be led by a thief is to offer up your most precious treasures to be stolen." "If you want to keep a secret, first you

must hide it from yourself."

Her notebook was filled with her small, tight handwriting. The smaller she wrote, the less likely people would be able to decipher her words. She would have written in code if she had known one. The boxes in storage might disappear at any time, but Sara could tell her daughter the stories.

Sara stared down at her fat elephant feet. How long had she been daydreaming? She desperately wanted to speak to her mother or Dr. Akin. Surely even he would help her now. She finished the apple and set the core on the tray. She stared at the thick, creamy milk. The sisters had never left before the glass was empty. If she didn't drink it now, they would force her to finish it when they returned. The milk would taste worse when it was warm and stagnant, and they'd bring another glass besides.

Why couldn't they give her water occasionally, or tea? Sara licked her lips. Her eyes were already growing heavy again, but she moved her legs over to the side of the bed and onto the floor. She slid her feet into the slippers. Her feet were so enormous, she had to use her hands to force the fabric aside to accommodate her swollen flesh.

She sat up, and the room spun like she was drunk. She closed her eyes. "You can do this," she whispered. She opened her eyes and waited until the room stood still. She grabbed the headboard and pulled herself up. Her legs shook, but she could not bear another sip of that disgusting milk. She grabbed the glass, and she lurched forward. How long did it take for her to cross the fifteen feet or so to the bathroom? Each step felt like she was pushing her clumsy bulk through water.

Finally, she stood in front of the sink. She poured the milk down the drain, surprised to hear her satisfied grunt. She rinsed the glass, then filled it with cool water. She drank it greedily. Even this minor task exhausted her. She yawned and leaned against the sink, preparing for the journey back to bed. *She had to get out. But how?*

The sisters locked the door. She walked slowly to the window that faced the street. It was a straight drop to the ground three floors below. There was no tree nearby, assuming she could maneuver her bulk onto the roof without falling.

She inched her way toward the closet door and opened it. The backpack was still there.

She bent down, bracing against the wall for balance. The effort was almost too much but she had to know, had to be sure. She opened the zipper and felt inside. Yes, the almanac was still there.

Her fingers continued hunting. So was the envelope. Sara pushed the backpack inside the closet and covered it with a blanket.

She retraced her steps in what felt like slow motion. When she reached the bed, her head pounded in time with her heartbeat, the strain behind her eyes so intense that she longed to submerge her body in the nearby quarry. What if she could float? Would that relieve any of this overwhelming pressure? *Big fish, little fish, swimming in the water.* She closed her eyes, and for a while, she dropped into the relief of sleep.

***

Sara recognizes her mother's gait, but she is too far away to see clearly. Then her mother walks toward Sara, holding a string tied to a balloon. Sara gasps. The glowing orb isn't a balloon. It's the moon.

"How?" Sara asks.

Her mother shakes her head. No questions. She hands Sara the string. Panic rises in her chest. How can she hold the moon? Sara takes the string, and the moon floats high in the sky.

Her mother turns and walks away, and tears slide down Sara's face. She knows it is a dream because she can't cry or sweat and barely pees now. It's as though her body has forgotten how to release water.

And then, in the way of dreams, she's at the quarry outside of town. She's been here.

Dreamed this dream before. She follows Ana up the cliff, her sister's skinny legs and tan skin a beacon.

Ana is only eleven, and Sara is technically an adult, but her younger sister is fearless. They stand at the edge of the cliff, staring down at the water below. Ana's friends and some of their brothers and sisters swim, others float on tubes or rafts. They peer up at the cliff, waiting expectantly. "She's not going to do it," a voice calls out. "She's afraid," another agrees.

Sara stands at the edge, feeling all that space below her like a void. While she tries to convince herself, Ana leaps, the sparkles in her purple swimsuit flashing. She takes risks Sara is too afraid to face. It's humiliating to be shown up by her kid sister.

"You can do it," Sara whispers to herself. "You can do it."

But she finds herself cursing under her breath as she climbs backward off the cliff to the good-natured teasing of Ana's friends in the water. Sara's knees are chalky with dust and bruised from the rocks. She wades into the water from the shore near the cave instead. She enjoys the sensation of floating, waves slightly rocking.

When she opened her eyes, she was in her room, staring up at the ceiling fan. *Dun-dun, dun-dun.* It was dark. The moon hung low and yellow outside her window. Full and heavy, like her. Slowly, it dawned on her that it was late. Why had no one come? Dinner should have been here by now, along with the droning prayers and the faint scent of sweet perfume.

Dun-dun … dun-dun … dun-dun. The fan spun, the hitch in the blades matching the pulsing behind her eyes. *Dun-dun … dun-dun.* The stairs creaked, and Sara started in bed. Shadows danced across the walls.

The steps continued in an odd, uneven tempo. It did not sound like either of the sisters. Sara's pulse beat faster. *Dun-dun … dun-dun … dun-dun.* Her head would explode or implode, she wasn't sure which. She almost didn't care as long as the pressure finally released its vice on her eyes, her temples.

"Who's there?" she called out, her voice barely above a whisper.

The strange, halting gait continued. A key rattled in the lock. Sara shoved her notebook under her pillow. The door creaked open, and Sara squinted at the shadow in the doorway. The woman standing there looked both familiar and like a stranger. Dark circles marked the skin under Ana's eyes like bruises. Her brown hair hung oily and lank near her face. And her sister looked strangely deflated.

"Ana?" she said uncertainly, her chest releasing in relief. Ashley had said her sister would come, hadn't she? Sara forgot everything these days.

Ana smiled. The planes and hollows on her sister's face glowed in the moonlight. It was like watching a skeleton grin. Sara shivered. Ana entered the room with that strange, unsteady gait. She carried a tray and the weight seemed almost too much for her.

"You look terrible," Ana said with deadened eyes.

"Please, I need your help." Sara held up her unrecognizable hands. "No one has checked my blood pressure in days. The sisters won't tell me where mom is, or where you were. They pray and pray but won't send anyone to help me. And Ana, they said something about adoption."

Ana made her way haltingly to the bed. Her clothes were so baggy they floated around her like a tent. She set down the tray with a bowl of tomato soup, a large piece of homemade bread, a glass of milk, a brown bottle, and a butcher's knife.

"What if there was no one to help you? What would you do then?" Ana made a noise then, a combination of a laugh and a sob, and the hair on Sara's arms rose.

"Where have you been? Where is Mom?"

"It's nice to see you too, sister. And I'm fine, why thank you." Anna collapsed onto a chair next to the bed, wincing. "Are you all right?" Sara asked.

"I," Ana's voice grew strangely flat. "I lost the baby."

"I'm so sorry." Tears should have filled Sara's eyes, but there was nothing.

Ana's pregnancy had advanced so much further than before. That made the loss even worse. No doubt Ana thought this time would be different.

"Mom said the baby was older than she'd thought. Almost six months."

Ana said this as if reading a list. No feeling, no inflection. "Charles said it's God's will," Ana continued bitterly. "He says I'm not supposed to question God's plans, but why does He give me these babies only to take them away?"

Ana's restless eyes searched Sara's face, then the walls, as though she could find the answer in the attic bedroom. Ana held up her palm and stared at it. "I held that tiny body in one hand. How could something be so small and perfect, and so broken?" Ana sobbed. "Charles wants to try again."

"You need time to heal." Sara licked her dry lips. Charles had no heir. Wives and daughters could not inherit under the new laws. His family's property and any wealth he had would be forfeit to the government if there were no males to inherit.

"It doesn't look right for the pastor, the spiritual father of our community, not to have any children of his own." Ana's voice broke. "He said it isn't right." Ana's voice grew louder with each word.

"You don't have to yell. I'm right here."

Ana reached toward the tray. The metal gleamed in the moonlight. Sara's pulse picked up again. *Dun-dun ... dun-dun ... dun-dun.* "What's the knife for?" There was nothing on the tray that required cutting.

"I started to understand when I was downstairs getting your food ready. I started to put it all together."

Sara took a deep breath. "God doesn't want you to create another life if it kills you, Ana. That's a bad deal." Her baby sister was still in there, inside this exhausted, confused shell. The girl who would jump, laughing, before the force of her body smashed into the water, creating waves that swept over her friends.

"Easy for you to say. You've only been married, what, two years? And Matthew was home on leave for only three days, and you still ended up with a baby." Ana sounded accusatory.

"Not yet." Sara said grimly.

"I've sinned. I'm being punished." Ana's shoulders shook. "Oh, Ana. Come here."

Ana moved the chair closer to the bed, wincing. Sara kept an eye on the knife as though it were a snake in the garden. "Before, you would have been able to go to a doctor, and they would have told you why you're having a hard time. There's probably a physical reason.

It has nothing to do with so-called sin. It could even be Charles, not you."

Ana stared at her, eyes gleaming with tears. "Don't say that."

"What"

"You'll be punished if anyone hears you. More than we already are."

"You're the only one here. And what do you mean? Who's being punished?"

Ana crossed her fingers, a strange custom among the women in town. It was meant to ward off evil, but Sara remembered it as a childish wish for good luck or to cover your tracks if you were fibbing. *It's a dumb superstition,* Sara told herself. But superstition was dangerous these days. Superstition could kill you.

Ana bit her lip, so dry and cracked it started to bleed. "She brought it on herself," she whispered.

"Who?"

"On the second night, Mom said there wasn't a heartbeat anymore, but I hadn't started to miscarry yet. She told Charles I could get an infection if she didn't do something, and he said yes. Do it. So, she gave me medication." Ana picked up the knife and ran her thumb along the edge of the blade. A fat drop of blood dripped onto her leg, staining her loose pants.

"Afterward, he asked how soon we could try again. Mom explained how long I would need to recover. But she said I needed time to heal emotionally too, not only physically. I hadn't even stopped bleeding and he was talking about having another baby. But Charles wouldn't listen. And Mom got mad. She yelled something like, 'Ana's not a walking womb.'" Ana's thumb was still bleeding. She left a bloody thumbprint on her pants.

Sara's face and scalp tingled. *Dun-dun...dun-dun.*

"Charles lost his temper. He said he hadn't believed the rumors about her until then." "What rumors?" Sara squeezed her pounding temples.

"Mom shouldn't have had that medication to begin with. It's used for abortions."

They had stopped the criminal trials for possession a couple of years ago, but that had been because no one had access to those medications anymore. Or so Sara had thought.

"Ana, please. Where's Mom?"

"She broke the law, and she made me break it too. I've sinned, and I'm the pastor's wife," Ana said helplessly. She still held the knife in one hand, and now she picked up the brown bottle in the other.

There was something ominous about the way Ana stared at it, as though studying the label. Sara's mouth was dry. She swallowed loudly. Her sister had not answered her question.

Ana stared at the knife and the bottle. "I'm not sure which of these would be better."

Better for what, Sara almost said, but she was afraid to know the answer.

"This morning, Charles called your doctor. He described your symptoms, said we had lost our physician's assistant. Lost," Ana laughed maniacally. "As if we misplaced her somewhere. Dr. Akin is coming here tomorrow to do an emergency C-section."

Sara's body flooded with relief. It was a physical sensation, as though cool water had been poured over her flaming face, her scalp. She breathed out. Her sister was distraught, her mother had maybe been arrested, but help was coming. "Thank God," she said.

"I wouldn't go thanking Him yet," Ana said, with that strange skeleton smile. "Charles asked Christina and Ashley to take care of you. They've been giving you this." Ana lifted the hand holding the bottle. "They left instructions in the kitchen. I was supposed to put it in your milk. They've sedated you so you wouldn't cause any trouble."

Sara looked at the glass on the tray. Milk was good for mothers, they said.

"I found a list downstairs. They've been keeping track of the laws you've broken. If you survive surgery, I think they'll put you on trial. It looks like they're building a case against you."

Suddenly, two thoughts connected in Sara's brain. "Ana, the sisters said that Charles wanted to adopt my baby. Is it because he's going to put me on trial?"

"Adopt," Ana repeated. "Why would we adopt your baby? Even if," she paused. "the worst happens, Matthew would still be the father."

"Charles didn't say *we*. He said *he*," Sara whispered.

Silence as Ana frowned, then connected the dots. "I believed. I believed it all, and it didn't make a difference. Eventually, Charles will figure out a way to marry someone else. Someone who can have babies. But until then, he'll have yours." Ana stared at the brown bottle in one hand and the knife in the other. "All I've ever wanted was to be a wife and a mother. But I'm not a walking womb. I'm a walking tomb."

From Ana's tone, Sara knew this was important, a piece of the terrible puzzle her sister had become. But she struggled to follow the words. Ana kept changing the flow of her conversation; it was like trying to hold water in her hand.

"While I was in the kitchen, I tried to think of a way. I tried and tried. But I couldn't." Ana squeezed the bottle tightly. "So I started thinking, maybe it would be better if it all just stopped. We could make it stop." Ana held out the bottle and the knife to Sara like an offering. "What do you think? I'll let you pick first."

Sara sucked in her breath so fast she made a whistling sound. She sat up, legs trembling. "Whatever you're thinking, no."

"That's your decision then?" Ana waited patiently, her face calm.

Sara stood, but her knees buckled, and she crumpled to the floor. "Ana, please." Sara had started to understand. Ana could not do the one thing women were supposed to do in this world. So she would leave it. She would take the leap like she always did.

"Will you forgive me?" Ana's eyes shone with tears.

"Yes. Of course, I forgive you. But you don't have to do this."

The church bell began to toll. Sara held her breath. *One,* a long pause. *Two.* The slow tolling continued for sixty seconds. One, two. A pause. One, two. A guilty verdict.

"Why are they ringing the bells?" Sara whispered. "Mother's trial," Ana said quietly.

"They'll only punish her, make her an example. She's the only medically trained person in town," Sara said urgently.

"You know what the bells mean," Ana said. Her voice sounded strangely calm, but she set the bottle down on the nightstand and reached for Sara's hand.

They grasped each other, their fingers intertwined. Ana's hand was shaking so much that Sara's whole arm vibrated.

"We've got to get out of here," Sara said. "And go where?"

"Anywhere." Sara remembered the backpack and her mother handing her a balloon that was the moon in the dream. But that memory dissolved almost as soon as she remembered it. She had to go now. She had to get out. "Ana, please."

"There's nowhere to go, Sara. There is no help." Ana started laughing then, but tears streamed down her face. Like the sun shining while it rained. Ana put the knife next to the bottle on the nightstand, released her hand, then climbed into the bed, taking Sara's place. "If you stay here, the doctor will come. I think they're going to let you die. But if you don't die, then you'll go to trial. Either way, they'll take your baby. And there's nothing we can do to stop them. But there's one thing I can do. Lock me in. Maybe I'll confuse them enough to buy you some time."

Sara crawled closer to the bed. She knelt and reached for her sister's hand. It felt like crossing a chasm, but finally, her fingers reached her sister. She squeezed the fingers clumsily and kissed the tips. Ana's thumb was bleeding again, and Sara counted the drops as they fell. One, two, three. Soon they would dry into a stain on the rug. She stared at Ana. For how long she wasn't sure; time had become so blurry. But she had to go. Someone would come soon. The sisters, Charles, someone.

"What if there was someone who would help us?" Sara said.

Ana said. "After you leave, I'll take the sedative. I won't make you watch." Sara started to tell her about the almanac, the address, but Ana shook her head.

"Don't say it. I'm not sure how long this sedative takes. If I don't know where you're going, then I can't tell anyone."

"Please," Sara thought she would cry now, but nothing came. "I'd hurry if I were you. My keys are in my purse downstairs." "I love you, Ana."

"And I love you, sister."

Sara reached behind Ana and pulled the notebook from under the pillow. She kissed her sister's forehead. Then she crawled to the closet, grabbed the backpack, and hoisted it onto her back. She used the wall to stand, shaking, and walked slowly into the hall. She closed the bedroom door behind her and fumbled the key into the hole. She didn't know how much of a head start she would get. Everything had to look the same. They had to believe she was still locked in the room.

What if Ana was wrong? Her sister was distraught, grieving. But Sara hadn't imagined the bells. She hadn't imagined the sisters saying that Charles would adopt her baby.

She would walk downstairs. She would open the envelope in the car and see if there were any directions. If there weren't, she would drive to the address printed on the front.

What if there was no one there? Or what if Ana was right, and no one helped her?

Then maybe she would go to the old quarry, walk into the cave veined with quartz, and ease herself gently into the water. She would float and stare up at the moon until the terrible pressure in her head eased. She would say goodbye.

Sara walked toward the stairs slowly. The dizziness hit her like a wave, and she closed her eyes until it passed. She would climb the cliff. No one would be there to see her, but this time, the last time, she would be fearless like Ana. She would jump.

But not yet. Her mother had left her this backpack, a small glimmer of hope. She was too dizzy to walk down the stairs. Sara turned and took a deep breath, preparing to crawl down the stairs backward. She knew she could do it. She'd had a lot of practice climbing off the cliff.

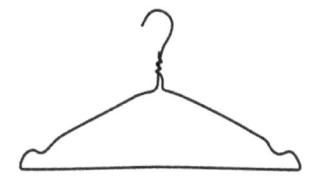

The Three Undoings of Della Rae- Sabrina Voerman

1693

A grey mist wafted around the wooden structure that held two people. The first was a man clad in black with his face covered to protect his identity. The legal crime he was about to commit required his protection and safety; after all, being chosen to execute a woman of barely eighteen might stir up some resentment from the villagers. His face was covered, but in a village as small as this, it was easy enough to determine who was behind the executioner's mask.

The second person on the wooden gallows was Della Rae Matheson.

A gentle breeze knocked the bell above her head. Every few seconds the metronomic rhythm of the soft clanging sound reminded her that she had to breathe. All the eyes of the villagers were on her; she wasn't looking through the crowd for a face that didn't hate her for what she had done. There would be some faces of sympathy and understanding—very few, but they would be there hidden among the sea of disgust. Many who endured the pain of childbirth would know why she did what she did. Although that did not excuse her for turning to the forbidden, a handful wouldn't hate her in death.

She made peace with that.

As she scanned the crowd through bleary, tired eyes that hadn't seen sunlight in a fortnight, she saw Isabel Curie in the very back. She was easy to spot, for she had a distinct look in her eyes; one was milky and blind. Her brown hair framed her face but the scar on her face was on full display, not a single curl covered that mark. Clad in a rich red velvet cloak, the woman everyone knew as a witch watched the procession with pensive eyes.

Della Rae thought she saw a glimmer of despair as Isabel clutched the infant to her body.

"Miss Matheson, daughter of the late Errol Matheson, you have been found guilty of conspiracy to murder, conspiracy to corrupt public morals, and witchcraft," the prosecutor said over the hum of conversation in the crowd. His words brought forth gasps and even shrieks.

Della Rae rolled her eyes—despite standing with a scratchy rope around her neck, she couldn't believe these people. She turned to witchcraft not to cause trouble, but to get even.

What else was a girl supposed to do?

Ten Months Earlier

Della Rae's hand was so small inside Theodore's. As he guided her to the barn under the moonbeams, she felt everything inside of her body ignite. The forbiddance of the act they were about to perform made every nerve light up. With each step, Della Rae's heart skipped with elation.

The barn came into sight under the milky night sky. It was autumn, and Della Rae had just turned seventeen. She knew her father was going to marry her off to Theodore Smith, which is why she was hand-in-hand with him, headed towards the safety of the barn where they could see just how far past kissing they would go. His hands had roamed her body over her dress and pinafore in the past, but tonight, she wanted to go further.

"Why wait?" Theodore had asked during a blessedly unchaperoned moment between them a fortnight ago. They had been skipping rocks along the riverbank just behind the old schoolhouse. "We already know they're going to have us wed, live together, build our lives together…Don't you want to know what it is all about?"

She did. Sara, Della Rae's best friend, had done it with Joel that summer. She told Della Rae all about it and how amazing it was. Della Rae had wanted to know what it was all about, and she did love that warm, fuzzy feeling she got whenever she was around Theodore. Sara and Theodore made excellent points, but the important thing was that Della Rae wanted to do it.

Theodore pushed open the barn door, which creaked ever so slightly. He released her hand as he dug through the musty hay looking for the ladder to the loft. When he unearthed it, he steadied it, and reached his hand towards Della Rae.

She took it and followed him up to the loft. The quiet peacefulness of it washed over her. How many hours she spent up here hiding away from chores, hiding from her parents, crying after her mother died. This place was a haven, and she was thankful to share it with Theodore. He laid a blanket down for them both, and in clunky, awkward movements, they began to unlace, unbutton, and unbuckle.

The first undoing of Della Rae was done at the hands of a boy she loved.

Della Rae was wrapped around Theodore; her skirts were rumpled, and her hair was disheveled. He stroked his thumb over the curve of her hip, over and over again to the beat of their hearts as they slowed back down. There was hay in his hair, and Della Rae was certain there was more in hers. For the first time, he saw her without her hair braided and pinned up, hidden by a bonnet. He got to see her in her purest, rawest form. Leaning in, Della Rae kissed him on the nose.

Theodore opened his mouth to say something, and Della Rae thought she knew what it might be. Before he had the chance to get it out, the barn doors rattled before bursting open, giving them only seconds to pull clothes back on. Della Rae's brown eyes took in the scene before her. Her father came barrelling in at full speed, his rifle in hand—his eyes were burning holes into Theodore, who was trying his best to cover Della Rae, to shield her from whatever evil her father was about to unleash.

"Della Rae, get down here right now," her father shouted. "Get away from that boy."

"Father, please! He didn't do anything wrong!"

Her father only laughed and repositioned the gun. "Get down here, both of you."

There was nothing they could do but oblige. With no escape from the loft, the only way down was into the firing line. Della Rae did her best to make herself decent, but her clothes were rumpled and her skin had a sheen of sweat—it was no secret what she and Theodore had done that night. She wouldn't change it, what they had done, but had she known that this would be the outcome, she would have done things differently.

At the base of the ladder, she watched as Theodore climbed down behind her. His hands were shaking, and she noticed that he hadn't done up the buckles of his boots. His nerves were too much, she could see that in the way he moved. Della Rae wanted nothing more than to wrap herself around his body, to protect him from whatever her father might do. She feared that she would never marry Theodore now. She heard of girls who laid with boys and had to marry them because no one would want to touch a girl who had been touched by another boy. Della Rae didn't feel dirty, except for the hay stuck to her body.

Though no part of her believed in the god she was told to pray to and obey, she asked for one little thing from Him; she asked that Father would still allow her to marry Theodore.

Instead, he pulled the trigger.

Nine Months Later

Della Rae was bursting at the seams. Her feet were struggling, feeling like they were about to pop under her weight. The baby inside of her was going to be the death of her, she thought. The moonlight overhead was bright, the sky was hazy dark, and the stars were being playful. It was the cusp of the solstice, and everything felt warm and bright. Except Della Rae, who brought with her a shaken look in her eyes everywhere she went. Whenever she was allowed out, she was hissed at, called a hussy, a tramp, a whore.

Some people blamed her for using her feminine wiles to seduce Theodore and trick him into bedding her. They accused her of laying a trap for him, knowing her father would kill him. No one seemed to blame her father, who was the one who pulled the trigger on that loaded gun.

No matter which way they spun the web, it was Della Rae's fault she was pregnant, and that Theodore was dead.

She wove through the woods to the cabin and its owner. Even in the moonbeams it was hard to see; the blackened colour of the building was coal-like. Only a flicker of light at the door, a lantern left on for the lost girls like Della Rae. The beacon of hope was hardly a light at all, Della Rae discovered, but rather a glass jar of fireflies. The jar rested on the steps in front of the A-frame cabin, and the fireflies lingered within. Della Rae got closer, curious to know why the fireflies would stay in the jar when they could fly, go anywhere, far, far away from this place.

Inside the jar was a slug with half its body missing. The gentle smell of tiny death wafted to her nose as she got too close. The fireflies feasted upon the slug, ravenous, starving, gluttonous.

"There are two ways to train something," a soft, feminine voice said. Della Rae snapped her head up from where she was crouched and spotted Isabel Curie. "Food and pain."

Della Rae stood up too quickly; her head began to spin, and she clutched the porch beam for support.

"You've taken a very large risk coming here, especially in your condition," Isabel noted, leaning against the doorframe and crossing her arms over her chest. She was lithe, just a waif of a woman, only a handful of years older than Della Rae. Shunned for her trickery in school, cast out for voicing her beliefs and views in a world that didn't want to hear anything on the lips of women other than *Yes, sir*.

"I need your help, Isabel," Della Rae managed to squeak out.

Isabel looked her up and down, then shifted her body so there was just enough room for Della Rae and her big belly to squeeze in through the door. Della Rae paused; there was no going back once she entered that house. All the horrible accusations the villagers spat at her would become true.

Della Rae stepped into her second undoing.

Inside the cabin was warm. Though no fire was going, there were lanterns all about. Satchels made of leather spilled out dried flowers on tables, books were open and filling the room with their scent and knowledge.

"Sit, you will be more comfortable," Isabel said. They both took a seat at the table. A loaf of bread sat in the center, and Isabel began to tear off chunks. She buttered one and handed it to Della Rae, who went to eat without thought. As the smooth goat-butter hit her lips, she stopped. Isabel smiled, showing soft crow's feet at her eyes. She was truly beautiful, despite the scar that marred the right side of her face, and the milky right eye. "I am not training you with food, do not worry."

Della Rae's shoulders loosened noticeably.

"You listen well," Isabel said. "This is good. But please, eat, we share a meal under my roof, and you will be protected from any harm here."

Della Rae nodded, and the two of them ate their buttered bread. When only crumbs remained on Della Rae's dress, and her fingers and lips were slick with grease, their work began.

"I am going to ask you something, Della Rae," Isabel said. "I want you to answer with the first thing that comes to mind."

"Okay."

"Why are you here?"

Della Rae hesitated for only a handful of seconds. Then, it sputtered from her lips. "I want my father to feel the pain I feel."

In the faint light it was hard to tell, but Della Rae was certain that Isabel Curie's smile was devious. "In six days, you are going to give birth."

"Six?"

"Yes." Isabel nodded, then continued as though she hadn't been interrupted. "The pain you will feel is going to be excruciating. Like nothing you have ever felt before. It is a pain that only people like us can feel, a pain put upon us whether we want it or not. We are breeders to them, nothing more. Remember that. Then, when your child is swaddled and given back to you, they will tell you that you are weak.

When tears fall from your tired eyes, they will say you are emotional, fragile, hysterical. They do not know what pains you suffer, have suffered, and will continue to suffer. They will not care that you lost your lover to violence and a man's hatred for your freedom. They will not care that your body has been altered forever. They will not care that the exhaustion that will follow you for the rest of your life will break you down. They will add it to the list of reasons why you, a woman, are weak."

"That's not fair."

"No."

"How can we change it?"

Isabel smiled wryly, and did not answer the question. "You wish the pain you have and will suffer upon your father, yes?"

"Yes."

"I cannot change the mindset of generations of belief, but I can do this for you." Isabel got up, began riffling through shelves, pulling jars, and emptying satchels. In a mortar and pestle, she ground this concoction in a matter of minutes. The dance she did with such fluid grace made her look like a dream to Della Rae. The house had been a total chaotic mess when Della Rae walked in, but seeing Isabel move with such ease and knowing where everything was, Della Rae saw the organization now.

It was so beautiful to watch a woman work like this.

Isabel placed a satchel into Della Rae's hand. "If you use this, there will be two costs."

"Two? I have no coin…"

"Bah," Isabel said. "Coin is a manmade thing, essentially useless except to keep the rich, rich and the poor, poor."

Della Rae blinked at Isabel.

"Never you mind. There are two costs, the one you know, and the one you don't." Isabel waited a beat, and when Della Rae said nothing, she sighed. "The one you know is your firstborn child."

"I beg your pardon…" Della Rae said without determination. She heard Isabel loud and clear, and the cost settled in her mind now. "You want my child?"

"I will care for your child, I will take care of her, I will show her a different way of the world that is uninfluenced by the parameters set upon us by people who do not understand us," Isabel said. "I will do nothing more than raise her to be the change we are fighting for."

"And if I say no…"

"When it is all over, when you've given birth, when you've given this powder to your father in six days…what do you think they're going to do?"

"Oh." Della Rae. "This is the other cost."

"Yes."

"If you take this powder tonight, what is done will never be undone. The cost is high, but progress blooms from the blood of those who say *no more*."

Six Days Later

Della Rae put the powder in her father's tea that morning. The sun had been caressing the sky with her rays all morning. With each contraction Della Rae tried her best to breathe through, the sun rose a little higher, as if excited to see the new life that would arrive. At midmorning, father had consumed all his tea, and Della Rae was alone in her bedroom, skirt pulled up past her knees, sweat dripping down from her hairline, streaking her face like tears. But she felt no pain as she endured childbirth.

The screams of her father filled the house. With each painless push, she could hear him whimpering in the other room, sobbing and letting out choked curses. As her daughter came into this world, she could hear bones cracking in the other room. As horrifying as it was, it made Della Rae smile. She thought of Theodore and the pain she felt as she watched him drop to his knees, hands touching his chest before he gazed down at the holes inside his body. He had been turning his head to see Della Rae when he collapsed. He'd fallen to his side, hazel eyes looking at her as he died.

The pain she felt as she saw her first love murdered at the hands of her father had been unfathomable. For months she wept while her body worked tirelessly to grow her daughter. She spent weeks throwing up, unsure if it was from the profound loss, or the pregnancy. All that pain, the past nine months, funneled now into her father.

She felt her child come into the world and she began to cry, but not tears of pain. It was clear to Della Rae that she would not have long. So, she leaned over her bent legs, picked up her child. Covered in blood and essence of womb, she was beautiful. When those bleary eyes opened, they were the same hazel as Theodore's. Della Rae soaked in this moment; she would have hours, days at most. She needed to bring her daughter to Isabel before the second cost came.

She cut the cord, cleaned herself and her daughter up, and on steadier legs than she'd ever had before, she left her bedroom. In the family room she followed the sound of moans. In a corner was her father, hardly a man at all now. She studied him, this twisted version of the man who dictated her life until today; what a pitiful sight.

"You disgust me," she said to him.

He whimpered from his twisted state on the floor. Leaned against the wall, he had blood seeping out of his chest from where Della Rae gave him her broken heart; for Theodore. His skin was bloated and bruised; for all the times he battered Della Rae over the years. And his hips were cracked, legs splayed at ungodly angles; for her daughter.

She stepped over his mangled, moaning form, and walked to Isabel's. Her third undoing was coming, and she would hold her head high as they put the noose around her neck.

Mercy- Kyra R. Tores

  They ripped us out of our homes and gathered us like livestock on the way to the slaughter, except slaughtering us would have been a kindness I knew they would refuse. They came in the night like burglars to steal anything we may have had that was worth any value, or like kidnappers in an attempt to take my sleeping child from his bed. Swoop him up in his slumber while he dreamt of trains and Legos, or whatever I imagine little boys might dream of. Instead, they came for me.

  There was a time not very long ago where this kind of thing was something you'd only see in movies or read about in books. It was horrifying, cruel, and unrealistic, but most importantly it was fiction. Today, it just means you're another victim who's been removed from your home, your family is ripped away from you, loved ones disappear forever, and you're left with this gaping hole where those things used to be. Now a nightmare lives instead.

I don't remember when it all began, because I've lost track of the days that eventually turned into months. I know it was the early morning after Thanksgiving when they broke into my home - correction - when they were *let* into my home and dragged me away in the middle of the night kicking and screaming.

"Lucas, stop them! Please! Why are you letting them do this?"

My husband of eight years, the father of our four-year-old son, stood near the front of our house and gestured to the men in the direction of the door.

I'd like to stand here today and say I'm surprised, but the truth is we should have all seen this coming, especially from those we never expected to turn us in. It was the ignorance and naivety that was holding us from the belief that those we loved would never wake up one day and betray us.

The details of why so many would turn their backs on their loved ones are each personal and full of reasons I'm sure they convinced themselves are valid ones, but it all started with the overturn of Roe V. Wade. It was a decision that shocked the nation and the entire world. The United States of America, "Land of the Free," was set back fifty years and was now nothing more than a country filled with fear and heartache.

This was a decision that affected anyone with a conscience.

"It wasn't always perfect, but there was progress. We had hope."

That's why the overturn was devastating.

"What's next?" women would ask when they began stripping us away.

"There will be consequences from this."

And they were right.

Women all over found themselves without available medical care to seek out the help they needed to prevent life from entering this world, and were being forced to carry unwanted regret. There were also plenty that never even consented to the punishment from the beginning. In time, their greatest worries and *what ifs* came to fruition when women lost their right to vote, taking any and all decisions based on their bodies and lives completely out of their hands.

As you can imagine, it escalated very quickly. Those with open and honest views about where a "woman belonged", were quick to put us back into the kitchen, while others believed we should be allowed to continue to work, contribute, and be an equal part of society. This was the new world and over time we would try our best to become accustomed to it, and some of us were even lucky enough to have a partner who didn't see us as something that was second in line or an afterthought.

Up until about a year or so ago, I was one of those people with a home, a family, the right to still work, who could drive; I was even allowed to think my own thoughts! Imagine that! That was all before I ended up in a place like this. One I would rightfully call a prison, but that's not the way they would sell it.

My name is Wren, but in here I'm just another number.

"4-1-5!" is what they call me when it's my turn to be seen by the doctor. There was a rumor on the outside that these were the numbers of how many of us they've taken since they started gathering women up like cattle, and those rumors were put to rest when a girl - no more than fifteen - was brought here right after me. Her name was Mercy, or *4-1-6,* and she was a fighter.

From the moment she walked through the thick, heavy door, I could feel the teen angst just oozing out of her. I remember being that age and feeling like everyone in the world was out to get me. Hating my parents, finding comfort in older boys who had other things on their mind, but I can only imagine what it must feel like when society really is out to get you, and mold you into something you were never meant to be. More than anything else though, I noticed the large, round belly she had her hand placed over as she entered the room.

"4-1-5, meet 4-1-6, your new roommate."

There wasn't anything to say, all I could do at the time was flash her a gentle smile that said I was sorry she was in here too. There should always be a rule that children should automatically be an exception to the horrors of the world, but unfortunately, they seem to suffer the most. Especially at the hands of those who are supposed to protect them. That was the case of Mercy, number *4-1-6*.

It took some time for the both of us to open up to each other. You'd think in a time like this, we would all learn to come together and find comfort in one another, but when you've been betrayed by the people you thought you could trust, it made trusting anyone else almost impossible. In time, those walls were broken down and we shared very similar stories. We were both betrayed by family, we were only children, and we were both pregnant. Only she was further along than I was, and she was getting closer to her delivery.

The only time we were apart was when we went to see the doctor. Routine check-ups to be sure both mom and baby were okay. The goal was to produce a healthy offspring and rumor was if you could birth a female, then they were that much happier with you. You might even gain some sort of favoritism around this place.

Weeks went by and Mercy was away more as she neared her due date, and her check-ups became more frequent. I began to fear for her and what it would mean when she did finally have her baby. She's just a kid, someone who should be sitting in a classroom and being voted prom queen, or singing in the school play. She deserved better than this and our government failed her.

On that final night she was asleep in my bed, something she'd done for weeks after we'd grown closer. She'd spent most of the evening crying after being told on her final visit to the doctor that she was 3 centimeters dilated.

"I can't do this, Wren. I just want my mom."

I held her and cried for the loss of her innocence and her youth. More than that, I cried for everything she was going to lose next.

Eventually her water broke, and she was taken away. It felt like a movie, everything was moving in slow motion. I think back on that morning often and wish there was more I could've done. Something to stop the men in white as they heard Mercy's moans of agony and came bursting through that same, thick, heavy door they brought her through and into my life weeks before.

Despite being forced to experience the intense pains of natural labor, Mercy remained a fighter. She kicked, screamed, scratched, and even bit her way to the delivery room. Even full of anger and fear, she remained an angel in her same white dress as they continued to drag her out of the room, but not before she looked back at me one last time and smiled.

"Thank you," was all she said before they took her away one last time.

***

I never saw Mercy or heard the numbers *4-1-6* again. I'm not sure where some of the younger girls go, or what happens to them once they deliver their babies. There's been talk about sending them away to other clinics who buy them at a higher price, or sending them to live with the new families who may want a sibling for the children they birthed in the future. All I know is this isn't the end for us. They can take our rights, they can take our ability to vote, to drive, to make basic decisions in our own lives, but they can't take our strength. They can't have our willpower to survive.

I know my fight ends here. I can feel the cramps and pressure of labor beginning, but each story told is a reminder that we pushed forward despite the world tearing us down before, and we'll do it again. The world will remember us.

And just like Mercy, I won't go down without a fight.

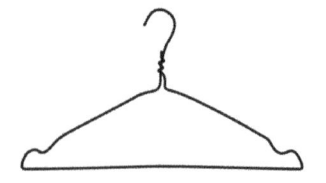

And They Shall Be Changed- Hazel Ragaire

They heard the women's prayers seething in anger and betrayal, worry and fear. They heard them in cars during commutes; they heard them whispering under bated breath with a baby riding a hip; they heard them in rooms haunted by 3 a.m.; they heard them over phone calls seeking strength and solidarity; they heard them from generations with wise-white hair or shaved, tattooed heads; they heard prayers raged to true lovers who raged right back.

So they rose.

They rose from pauper's graves, tattered sheath dresses trailing behind them.

They rose from family crypts in their Sunday finest.

They rose from Victorian graves, floating between the iron and stone mortsafes.

They rose from ditches, marking the spaces the living never found.

They rose from watery graves, free of the weight that bound their bodies.

They rose with broken bones and bruises no make-up could hide.

They rose with breasts or without them.

They rose from beneath wildflowers and trees and suburban tracts and skyscrapers, because the dead are buried everywhere if one looks deep enough.

Some prayers hold power. Tethered to the rage and fear and anger they felt, they faintly corporealized among the world again in solidarity. For some, little time had passed, but for others, their clothes spoke to centuries and centuries gone. And while the world's shimmer had lessened, and its skies grown foggier and its waters darkened, the patriarchy stood unchanged.

The oppressors, fists tight, reigned as if all homes, all boardrooms, all spaces existed only for them. Unrepentantly, they saw women as commodities, as replaceable things; one womb was as good as the next for housing their seeds. They worried that as women rose claiming agency, they would never want to bear patriarchy's children. For the patriarchy, NO possessed a double meaning: for men, it existed as a finality; they allowed women to only use it as a pause if at all.

Sensing the rising storm, fire crackling through the skies, for the sake of men everywhere those holding power gaveled it against females again, forcing women to bear every child, regardless of its conception story or risk to her mental, physical, and life-long well-being. Because the future that brings the patriarchy to its knees is one where women revolt, choosing themselves, announcing this choice with a Fury's thundering, "NO".

And so the risen listened and responded to the women's determination for bodily autonomy. They sought out the black robed and their acolytes, the devils in women's midst, and a great haunting began on a scale no imagination had yet dreamed.

For once, the patriarchy experienced hysteria.

The ghosts of women past stalked the patriarchy until nowhere was safe. Relentlessly, the women of before refused to release them even while they slept. Their drinks turned sour, and their nipples oozed. Fear channeled from the women's lived experiences entered their thoughts every minute of every hour. The patriarchy drowned in physical pain, enduring memories of surgeries sans anesthesia; the men would call out only to be disbelieved. Treasured objects in their lives went missing, and their private residences were as chilled as the morgues where women lay, unable to warm. The living stood by and watched these men and some women inch towards madness as the dead worked to shift the world.

    The dead's iridescent forms, sighted by peripheral blinks or hairs raising on one's arms, began to strengthen their outlines as the living believed. Billions of ghosts moved into every available space, murmuring, "Never Again", haunting everywhere they always should have been. Sometimes outlines merged and the ghosts walked with four sets of eyes, the shorter woman's protruding from the chest of the taller one. The patriarchy claimed mass hallucinations from contaminated water sources and struggled about their days. But the media outlets broadcasted faint outlines and the world watched the dead move among them. The living women saw and heard and knew they would rise and reshape reality. The dead thickened the air forcing the robed and their supporters to breathe them in. Leaving rest behind, the dead offered themselves as parasites for change.

    The robed walked, and felt unclean as an ashy miasma coated their skin. Centuries of dead haunted every step they took, anchoring into their bodies, worming their way through the skin and viscera. The miasma strengthened until resurrected women's souls destroyed patriarchy's agency blindingly, beautifully.

    The men breathed in this heavy air and often woke from bloody dreams sweating, knowing names of women long dead. They witnessed women's historic horrors at work or while driving or while gathering with the like-minded.

    In dreams they are female, wombs expanding, then painfully contracting as preventable sepsis sets in. In minutes their minds live through months forcibly carrying a fetus incompatible with life to birth it and endure its suffering, the hospital and funeral home's insurmountable bills a final, crushing weight. They experience the desolation at being denied gender affirming care. They double over in pain as an ectopic pregnancy goes untreated. Nightmares of patriarchy's own making transport them to realities unfolding as they slumber, of women seeking care, knowing one's body desperately requires experts' help, only to be turned away with murmers of, "I'm sorry, but you're not yet sick enough to treat" echoes for weeks and months before the mother, finally sick enough and close to death enough, flatlines on arrival and dies; toe-tagged, decorating a morgue filled with women whose stages of protruding bellies far outnumber any other patient class. Dead, these women, single or married, young or old, seasoned or new mothers rise and join the ranks of the haunting, forcing the robed to live their stories to their untimely conclusions since the sanctity of life applies to some instead of to all.

    Some of the patriarchy stops eating, seeing visions of bloodied women everywhere, even splayed upon their dining room tables as real as when the women's lives had ended.

    The longer they resist, the more they breathe, the more of the dead move in, relinquishing death's peace for agency's battleground, seeking homes in the patriarchy's brains and nervous systems, and ultimately every single cell. Tiny atoms of the risen women find purchase, anchoring down, sending tendrils of themselves into the living cells with one pure, coded intent: never again. Pure possession follows days later until the remaining robed and their supporters stop one day and walk, jerking feet forward, eyes frantically pleading, arms akimbo, heavy and unwieldy for the ethereal women now in charge. The living women and the men who stood beside them in solidarity stand watching as the Earth itself seems to still as those who had viewed them as lesser, as mere means to an end, as disposable, shuffle forward under their gaze; some of the patriarchy and its lessers stumble, knees cracking upon the pavement and no one helps them rise; the fallen's will abandons them and they remain where they lay, a testament to the beginning of the end. Their skin begins to smoke, growing translucent until breaking, releasing the wronged. And the patriarchy begins to fade, its members forgotten, their ashes carried by the wind.

    Slowly the remaining masses amble towards large structures: stadiums, convention centers, amphitheaters, auction houses, and fallow fields and they sit, immobile, staring.

    And sit, devoid of any agency of their own.

    The world watches, warned.

    Patriarchy's wronged immobilizes the last believers until the returned drain their will to endure or they repent, pledging to atone for their grievous wrongs knowing that they will never be alone in their bodies again. Settled, the dead nestle down into their hosts to guide the world to where it should have always been, for they have eternity, and these bodies will decay and set them free. For now, the returned will stay for change is slow, even for the best puppet masters. The risen are content to watch the weights bowing women's backs and hobbling their hands disintegrate so their sisters can rise and claim themselves.

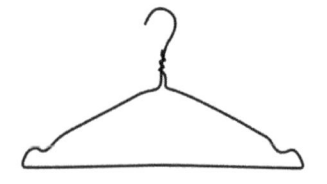

Go Down Swinging- Tiffany Michelle Brown

"That's impo—" My throat constricted. I tried to swallow, but my mouth had gone dry. "Impossible," I croaked so quietly, I was sure only I could hear it.

"Congratulations," Dr. Whiting said. "I'll want to see you on a weekly basis now, to track your health and progress."

"But I don't—"

Dr. Whiting met my gaze, and I snapped my jaw shut. The man radiated clinical coldness, but it wasn't simply his taciturn bedside manner that staid my protests. I could sense something else laying in wait beneath his starched doctor's coat, under his skin, rotting in the very heart of him. Something violent. I didn't want to awaken it.

I glanced up at the small circle of glass in the corner. The steady red light let me know, yes, recording was in progress.

Another reason to keep my cool. A shiver rattled down my spine at the thought of someone watching us from the comfort of another room.

"Smile," Dr. Whiting said, sliding forward on his cushioned stool to pat my leg. His palm was warm and heavy. I wanted to escape the weight of him by ramming my knee into his perfect, dimpled chin.

But I couldn't do that, could I?

"You're carrying the miracle of life." The doctor gave me an expectant look. He wanted me to be happy. Overjoyed. Elated that I was pregnant, despite the fact that I hadn't had sex with a man in five months.

And if I didn't give Dr. Whiting what he wanted during this appointment, how would I be punished? What injustices would I add to my mounting dystopian scorecard?

The past three months had been a veritable horror show. I'd lost so much so quickly. When our government banned access to abortion and I authored a scathing diatribe on social media, my bank balance mysteriously zeroed out. At the time, I thought it was simply an accounting error, so I called my bank, explained the situation, and got right back to expressing my disdain for social policies publicly. I attended a protest, yelling through a megaphone until my vocal chords were shot.

The day after the protest, my account balance was restored, but that's also when a black sedan rolled up in front of the house across the street. It didn't budge for a week, a man in sunglasses always behind the wheel. I called the police, but they never came. One morning, the car was gone, and though I was glad to see it go, I knew deep down in my bones that I was still being watched.

No. Nothing good could come of fighting the news of my pregnancy. I needed to act rationally, not emotionally. I gritted my teeth and forced my lips into a tight, unfeeling smile.

"Good girl."

Thank God, my middling compliance was enough. Dr. Whiting glided back over to his computer and started typing, allowing me some time to sift through the thoughts whirring around in my brain like a blender on high speed.

How the fuck had this happened? It had to be a false-positive, right? That was the only reasonable explanation.

You aren't living in a reasonable world, Haley. I shuddered, because my gut was right.

Four weeks ago, I'd been refused my birth control refill. When I asked the pharmacist why the request was denied, he didn't have an explanation and told me to contact my doctor's office. When I called, I was told my regular gynecologist, a gentle and progressive Middle Eastern woman, was retiring, and my new doctor would be Bradley Whiting, M.D.

This news didn't make sense. Dr. Khouri was vibrant and seemed young. She couldn't be approaching retirement age, could she? I reasoned that perhaps a family matter had drawn her away from her practice. Whatever the case, I knew I would miss her upbeat personality and dedication to the welfare of her patients. There was no way this Dr. Whiting guy could fill her shoes.

The receptionist let me know I was scheduled for an introductory appointment with Dr. Whiting the following day. I accepted, figuring I'd meet him, suffer through an initial exam, get my refill, and then ask for another gynecologist, preferably a woman. Oh, how wrong I was about that.

Seemingly overnight, all woman, queer, and BIPOC health providers were replaced with white, male counterparts. I started receiving messages that I was to report to my doctor's office biweekly, and if I missed an appointment, there would be consequences. Social media networks spontaneously went offline. So did the news. My phone was my last connection to the world, but I had no internet, just text messaging. I'd been thrown into a disconnected existence with no explanation.

And now I was pregnant. In a country that did not support a woman's right to choose. With no knowledge of how it had happened.

Dr. Whiting returned, holding a spiral-bound book out to me. I frowned and pulled it into my lap, surprised by its heft.

"This manual contains everything you'll need to know about your pregnancy," Dr. Whiting explained. "There's a schedule of appointments, nutritional requirements, dos and don'ts, everything to ensure this process goes smoothly."

This process? Heaviness settled into my gut like a stone. It was one thing to speak clinically. This was something else.

I flipped open the book to a random page, and bile immediately rose in my throat. According to this manual, I was to remain at home the next nine months, under surveillance, escorted out only for my medical appointments. Groceries would be delivered to my home, and I would stick to a curated diet designed to "support life". A crew would come to my house to dispose of anything that could threaten the viability of my pregnancy. As I read, the words blurred on the page.

My hands gave out, and the manual tumbled to the floor. Dr. Whiting swooped down to retrieve it. He set the manual on a nearby chair. "There, there," he said, gathering my hands in his. My stomach roiled in disgust, and I resisted the urge to crawl out of my skin. "I know this can be overwhelming, but soon you'll see what an incredible opportunity this is."

Opportunity? Was he fucking with me? It sounded like he was talking about a new job, not a—

Oh. Reality smacked me right in the jaw. *A new job. A mandated position.*

Gooseflesh sprouted across my arms.

This had been planned.

This had been…done to me.

I suddenly felt as if I was suffering from heat stroke. Woozy. Weak. Unable to function.

Now is not the time, Haley. You have to get out of here. You have to survive this.

Examination table paper crinkled between my fingers as my hands formed fists, and the sensation was enough to ground me. Now was not the time to crumble.

Fight, flight, or freeze, Haley. Which will it be?

Summoning every ounce of strength within me, I straightened my spine. Sat tall. Put on an air of ease like I would a coat. "I'm so sorry about that, Dr. Whiting. Even great news can be a lot to take in." The cheerful lilt I added to my voice felt like a splash of acid on my tongue. I hoped it sounded better than it tasted.

Dr. Whiting gave me a too-white, too-wide smile. "I completely understand. First time for you, right?"

"Yes."

"You're going to love it, trust me."

"I'm sure I will." The honey in my voice made me want to vomit. "I do have a quick question, doctor." I gazed down at my lap in a show of mock meekness. "I'm not entirely sure who the father is." A hot tear escaped my eye, and that small release of frustration felt like freedom. "Will there be a way to get a paternity test?"

"I'm afraid not."

I blinked at the rapidity of Dr. Whiting's response. The surety of it.

"Why not?" I asked. "I'd like to share the good news with the father."

Dr. Whiting reached out and tapped the cover of my pregnancy manual. "When you read this, it will all make sense. The father, whoever he is—" This motherfucker *winked* at me. "He's no longer an integral part of this equation. The *only* priority is in there." Dr. Whiting gestured to my womb.

Everything clicked into place. The inordinate amount of time my "pap smear" had taken during my first appointment with Dr. Whiting. The cream he'd used for my pelvic exam that had felt a good amount thicker than vaginal lubricant or petroleum jelly. The "see you again *real* soon" the receptionist had pitched my way as I left the medical office four weeks ago.

A river of sudden rage coursed through my veins, burning hot and rich and volatile. Something in my chest expanded and exploded.

I knew what I needed to do.

I moved as fast as hummingbird wings, launching myself off the table and toward my purse. I plunged my hand into its depths. Cold metal greeted my palm. As I extracted the knife, I clicked its switch, and the blade *whooshed* to attention.

I had no fear in that moment, only rage and malice and a hunger for revenge. I was a wounded animal ready to savage those who'd put me in harm's way. A person who had been targeted based on what I could provide, not who I was or what I wanted.

Dr. Whiting was on his feet now, his arms extended, palms to me, thinking his body would be enough to keep me at bay. Oh, how wrong he was.

I aimed for the pink flesh between Dr. Whiting's coat and the stubble of his five o'clock shadow. My body did not betray me, and I was immediately showered in viscous heat. Dr. Whiting dropped to the ground, hands scrabbling at his throat in an effort to staunch the jet of blood that poured from his severed carotid artery. I peered down at him, watching as he wheezed, his bulging eyes as big as plums.

"You will not force this on anyone else ever again." I dropped to my haunches. "Smile, Dr. Whiting. I know it's overwhelming, but it's such good news."

An alarm began to blare as the light exited Dr. Whiting's eyes. I stood and took a steadying breath. I rolled my shoulders back and turned to face the closed exam room door, my body vibrating with energy.

They were coming, Dr. Whiting's cohorts, I knew that. And when they did, they'd learn that women are capable of both the miracle of life and the gift of death.

I repositioned the knife in my hand, felt my fingers flex. I wasn't sure if I'd make it out of the office alive, but one thing was sure—if I had to go, I would go down swinging.

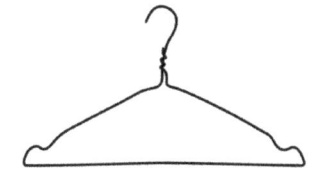

Witch's Heart- Stephanie Parent

The scent of burning flesh suffused the air.

Laura, who was vegan despite her mother's protests about protein and iron and the many needs belonging to the body of a teenage girl, couldn't stomach the smell. And so she'd wandered away from the last cookout-slash-first bonfire of the school year. She'd left behind her eleventh-grade classmates biting down on gristly hamburger patties, their hot dogs oozing ketchup like blood. Their chomping jaws and meat-flecked lips.

The farther she walked into the woods, where the leaves grew golden at their edges, like kindling touched by a match, the more Laura's discomfort drifted away. In a few weeks the trees would ignite with the New England autumn, blazing red and orange against air turned chillier with each lengthening night. Already, she shivered as the sun descended—

"Hey." The smoke-toned, very male voice turned Laura's shiver into a shudder. "Do you want my jacket? You look cold."

She glanced back to see Jake Harper in a T-shirt, holding his Southbury Torches football team jacket out to her. But when had Jake's voice grown so deep? And his biceps emerging from the shirt sleeves, flesh clinging to the remnants of a summer tan, looked bigger than they had just last week.

Maybe the twilight was playing tricks.

Jake's presence should have been a relief, but instead Laura's shudder wormed its way inside her, quickening her heartbeat. This was it: her teen movie moment. The first party of her junior year. She was the girl who'd never been kissed, wearing the effortless-looking-but-oh-so-carefully-chosen tank top and jeans, alone with a guy just a little more popular than her. Here they stood, beneath the cover of that massive oak tree Laura had known since childhood. The one with the knot in its trunk that formed the exact shape of a heart.

Above them, the moon rose heavy and full, competing with the last fiery rays of sun.

Before Laura could decide what to think or do, Jake was wrapping the jacket around her shoulders, his face close enough she could smell the beer and hamburger on his breath. He placed a finger under her chin and tilted her head up toward his, and she wondered if this was it, the moment, come so soon. Laura wasn't particularly attracted to Jake, but she couldn't deny the appeal of his dark eyes on hers as if she were something worth tasting, better than meat.

"Warmer now?" Jake asked, and gave her the same smile he did all the popular girls. This close, his gaze nearly smoldered. But then he let his hand fall.

Laura was left unbalanced, not knowing which way to go. She stumbled backward toward the old oak until—*smack*—the back of her head collided with scalding-rough bark. The world tilted, Jake's face a flickering patchwork of light and shadow; Laura blinked, and reality righted itself.

"You okay?" Jake said, and even though Laura wasn't, she nodded, in that automatic way girls were taught to do. He smiled again, flashing teeth that looked yellower than she remembered. Probably the twilight, or the beer. Softly, he whispered, "Good."

And then, before Laura could blink, it *was* happening—for real this time, his lips on hers but there was no teen movie soundtrack, no euphoric pop song, only the hollow whistle of the wind between branches far above. Laura reached for Jake, not sure whether she wanted to pull him closer for protection, or thrust him off.

Her hand met coarse fabric over a forearm, where Jake's flesh had been bare moments ago. Laura yelped into Jake's mouth and tasted breath that was rancid, like an animal's; breath from a mouth that had never met a toothbrush or dentist, and roiled like rot.

Laura's touch turned into a push.

"Hey," said Jake, that same smoky voice, "I know you want this. Come on, Laura, don't be a tease—"

Now that he'd stepped back, Laura saw the world twisting and transforming again around Jake's dark silhouette. The trees grew thicker, the branches more tangled; the path through the woods eaten up by foliage even as she watched. She could no longer see the peaked roofs of the houses back on the road.

"Jake," her voice trembled, "Jake, do you see—"

"I see you, sexy girl," said Jake's voice, but when he grabbed her wrists those long, coarse sleeves scratched at her like sparks. She pulled away, smelling a fire wilder than the cookout, inhaling cinders.

"Jake," she said, "something's burning. We've got to get out of he—"

"Quiet," he ordered—but only his voice was still Jake. Strange hands forced her back against the oak's trunk, strange teeth bit into her neck like meat, as the smoke swelled till Laura's eyes watered and burned. Thick, sooty panic invaded her lungs. Heat licked her skin everywhere the stranger-who-had-been-Jake touched. Laura pushed and swatted and clawed till she felt more animal than human, but the man was stronger, and soon the ashes had coated her insides and the world turned dark.

Laura's body fell limp against the old oak tree, as some part of her floated up, up above the branches. She watched her body and Jake's dissolve into shadows, a different vision arising in their place:

A history seeping out of the oak's bones.

***

Whenever Lucas neared the young oak with the heart-shaped knot in its trunk, his own heart beat faster. After his long journey through the woods, he was getting close. It was just like Bridget, to build her cottage as far into the wilderness as she could. Make men trek their way to her, if they wanted the treasures she could offer. And trek Lucas had, for the past hour, with the tomatoes and squash from his family's garden growing heavier by the moment. The sack *thump, thumping* like a drum against his back.

And then Lucas was past the oak, and the chimney of Bridget's homestead emerged from the treetops to beckon him on. No smoke rose from it today—it was much too warm for that, and if Bridget were to cook, she would light a fire outside. She'd bring out her cauldron and joke that she was one of the witches from *Macbeth*.

Yet when Lucas finally emerged into the September sun-dappled clearing, Bridget wasn't cooking. She was in her herb garden, skirt hitched up and bare knees in the dirt, wisps of midnight hair escaping the knot at the nape of her neck. No bonnet like the women in the village wore. Behind Bridget stood the little wattle-and-daub cottage she really had built herself—with some help from a few menfolk. As for how she'd repaid them, Lucas reckoned that wasn't any of his business, even if the rest of the settlement whispered and wondered.

Lucas didn't want to think about what Bridget might be doing with other men. All he wanted, in this moment, was to watch the way the sun lit her tan skin: her arms exposed nearly to the shoulder, the flesh peeking above her laced bodice, the liberties she could take out here with eyes so rarely upon her. Bridget was at least ten years older than the girls Lucas's own age, the ones he attended church with on Sundays—but those girls were like wavering candle flames compared to Bridget, the sun herself, blazing till he could feel her fire from across the yard.

Lucas dropped his sack of vegetables heavily enough to make Bridget turn his way. Hopefully he hadn't crushed the tomatoes—the overripe, bleeding fruit was the only payment he could offer her.

Bridget stood and smiled till faint lines crinkled around her eyes. "Lucas. Shouldn't you be tending your parents' fields on this fine afternoon? Or asking some pretty young thing to the church supper?"

"You could come with me to the church supper," Lucas blurted before he could stop himself.

Bridget shook her head, though the smile didn't waver. "Reverend Harper would spit on my face if he saw me within ten feet of his church." Her face tightened around still upturned lips. "He'd spit on me no matter where I was." She brushed her hands on her skirt, and Lucas breathed mint and rosemary, soil and sweetness. "But let's not talk about Reverend Harper."

Bridget drew Lucas closer with earth-stained fingers, and she kissed him, hard and long.

Later, they lay together on the straw mattress that seemed softer than silk in the afterglow. Lucas traced the sunlight where it sprinkled through the window and across Bridget's hair, her cheek, her chin. "Why did you never marry?" he asked, as he sometimes did, and Bridget offered her familiar answer:

"My soul is too wild and windblown for one man to hold." Her eyes gazed softly upon him, the shade of a fire contained in a hearth. "But isn't it time, Lucas, for you to look for a wife of your own?"

***

Abigail Harper should have been able to follow her best friend's directions, or to remember them, at least. She should have made it through the woods without getting lost and wandering in circles. If only her stomach wasn't heaving like a ship on a storm-tossed ocean, even after she'd emptied its contents twice this morning. Though she'd taken pains to hide her queasiness from her mother, the woman's sharp eyes had seen through Abigail's excuse about bringing some mending to Lucy's. Still, her mother had let Abigail go, with a disapproving shake of her head and a warning not to be too long.

If only Abigail's mind were not as upset as her stomach; if only the clouds inside her head were not expanding toward some inescapable storm. The trees blurred, her feet colliding with every stick and root as desperation met exhaustion—and then, she spied it, one clear sight before her. The heart-shaped knot in the oak, the one Lucy had told her to look for. She was so close; she would let herself shut her eyes and rest here, just for a moment.

When Abigail's eyes re-opened, a beautiful woman with dark hair and flame-colored eyes hovered over her. "Can you walk," the witch-woman said, "or do I need to get the wheelbarrow?"

Abigail stumbled to her feet and leaned on the woman, and together they made their way to the little cottage and gardens Abigail had heard so many rumors of. She was, perhaps, the only girl in the village who hadn't snuck out to spy on Bridget the sorceress, on the night of a full moon.

But then, Abigail was the reverend's daughter. The rules, the consequences, were more serious for her.

As soon as they entered the garden, a pungent odor invaded Abigail's nostrils. The scent of green growing things, powerful and inescapable. Doubling over, she tried to retch again, but had nothing left to expel.

Bridget wrapped a sun-warmed arm around Abigail's shoulder, a kindness her own mother would never have offered, and led her inside and sat her on a stool. Abigail stared into the swirls and spirals of the wooden table as, out of the corner of her eye, she saw Bridget moving about the kitchen and plucking bundles of herbs from the ceiling. The woman was stoking a fire, boiling water, before Abigail had the courage to say: "Aren't you going to ask me—"

"I know why you're here." Bridget tossed thick hair from her eyes. "You are not the first young girl to stumble her way to my home, clutching her stomach. A draught of pennyroyal and mugwort should be sufficient, as long as you are not too far along."

Abigail expected the tea to make her sick again, and perhaps later, it would; but for now the hot liquid soothed her throat and stomach and womb like Bridget's touch had minutes ago. The lulling lullaby of it made her speak what she should have kept to herself:

"It would have been all right." Abigail swallowed the last of the bittersweet brew. "I could have kept it, we could have wed"—she rested a hand on her belly, the way she had seen so many women in the village do— "except that he does not care for me. When he touched his lips to mine… It was as if he were forcing himself." The words brought the aftertaste of the morning's sickness to her tongue. "I believe he loves someone else."

Bridget placed her palm on the spot between Abigail's shoulder blades, melting away the tension there. "I could have loved him, though." The words slipped unbidden from between Abigail's lips. "I could have loved Lucas."

Bridget's hand fell away. The woman still smiled, but the flames in her eyes went dark.

***

That Bridget was the devil herself. Why else would she live out here in the forest's depths, with only wolves and demons for company? Why force a man—a *reverend*, even—to hike out here in this infernal Indian summer, with the sweat roiling under his starched collar till he thought he'd go mad if he didn't rip the fabric off? The gall of that woman—that witch—making him come to her.

And when Reverend Harper had passed the oak tree and reached the border of Bridget's land, land bought and planted upon with sin, she didn't even have the decency to stand and greet him. No, she just kept tending those vile herbs, though he was sure she knew of his presence.

Finally, the reverend cleared his throat, with all the authority he displayed before delivering a sermon. Bridget rose, slow as she pleased, and brushed her palms on her skirt before turning toward him. "As if you could ever make those dirty hands clean," he spoke.

"Reverend," Bridget replied in that siren-sweet voice of hers, "I did not expect a visit from you today."

"And I did not expect to hear that my daughter had come seeking your services."

If Bridget was surprised, her amber enchantress's eyes didn't show it. "I can never turn away someone in need of my help," she replied. "Surely you, a man of God, leader of your flock, can understand that."

"I understand nothing of your kind." He took in her wild black hair, the swell of her bosom over a shift much too low, the intoxicating scent of flowers and herbs. He had not meant to indulge carnal appetites today, had intended only to admonish her for the rumors sweeping the village; but if he did not divest himself of his collar and shirt immediately, he truly would rip them off, and then his wife would know.

As always, the moment the reverend touched the witch's flesh, she transformed him into an animal. Possessed, he yanked her hair and bit and scratched at her skin and finally invaded her as if they were two wild beasts in the woods. And then, as always, the second he had expelled himself, he spat his disgust right onto Bridget's face, and she lay there and took it.

And that was why she deserved such ill treatment: she was a filthy whore.

As the reverend rose and dressed himself, Bridget watched from her bed with a face void of all emotion, his spit still glistening on her cheek. What he'd done was his right, he reminded himself—it was the payment he took for allowing this woman to exist outside of his congregation's rules, outside of good Christian morals. But her blank, unblinking gaze still felt like judgment upon him.

"You went too far, helping Abigail," he told her before he departed. "I will not give you another warning."

***

Prudence Harper marched through the woods with her back ramrod straight and her shoulders broad and open, the same way she would walk up the aisle at church. She hoped no prying eyes followed her, but one could never be too careful. The reverend's wife couldn't show weakness for a single moment.

Even if she did, in fact, feel weak, because the truth was that she was lost in this forest, and the afternoon shadows grew longer.

Prudence had not asked directions to the witch-woman's home—she'd wanted no villagers to know of her destination. But if Prudence could oversee a household of two sons and three daughters, and still appear beside the reverend at church every Sunday with nary a wrinkle on her collar or a stain on her skirt, then surely, she could find some hut in the woods.

Yet now she'd passed that same oak tree with the ugly, lumpy knot protruding from its trunk for what had to be the third time. She was going in circles.

Prudence huffed and wiped sweat from her brow, wishing she could throw her bonnet off and let the cool breeze run through her hair.

"Looking for someone?" Startled by the words, Prudence let out a yelp so wild it mortified her. She turned toward a sight more feral than her own sound: a woman with long, uncovered hair and eyes the color of a wildcat's.

"So you're Bridget," Prudence spat. Her indignation had smoldered the entire way here, and now it sparked to life. "You're the one corrupting our young womenfolk. Making them think they can cavort as they please, and you'll magick their sins away. Well, I won't stand for it any longer."

Bridget's eyes widened, untamed and alarmingly beautiful. "You're Abigail's mother," she said more quietly. "And the reverend's—"

"Wife. His good, Christian *wife*." This woman needled at Prudence so. How dare she look so lovely and self-satisfied, out here all alone. "We live an upright existence, unlike some women who cast their sin—"

"If you're looking for sin," the venom in Bridget's voice now matched Prudence's, "you'd best start in your own home."

The blood heated in Prudence's veins till she thought it might boil over. "My Abigail is a good—"

The witch had the gall to chuckle. "Oh, I'm not talking about your daughter. She's a sweet young thing, if a bit naïve." Bridget licked her lips, rolling words over her tongue before she expelled them. "It's the reverend whose whereabouts you might question."

The nerve of this devil-woman was too much. Prudence might burst right into flame if a breeze didn't come cool her. "What in Heaven's name do you mean?" she demanded.

And Bridget told her.

***

On the night the full moon pierced through the clouds, Bridget knew they were coming for her. She could smell their approach in the wind like burning embers. Maybe she should have packed her dearest possessions, set off into the darkness of the trees with no destination; but she wasn't capable of outrunning fate. Bridget was not a witch, had made no deals of the devil, yet she knew that much.

If only, when Prudence confronted her, she'd managed to hold back her angry words. Bridget couldn't even say who she was so vexed at. Lucas had only done what she'd told him, and found a nice village girl. And the reverend had only behaved according to his own nature. No use blaming a monster for acting like one.

Perhaps Bridget was furious at a world where, for a woman like her, the only possible ending was in stomping boots and flaming torches.

By the time the men reached her, Bridget was outside waiting for them. She stood tall, chin lifted, though she wanted to crumple like a piece of parchment. The reverend led the pack, holding his torch high so his visage transformed into a flickering patchwork of light and shadow, more beast than human.

Bridget was glad for the blazing of his torch, the way it blurred the rest of the men into one writhing mass behind him. This way, she could not distinguish their faces. Could not determine how many of these men had brought her gifts, had shared her bed or just a smile, a touch.

And then Reverend Harper thrust his torch into the hands of another man, a shadow. The reverend marched closer, looming over Bridget, his hair stinking of grease and his breath rancid. He grabbed her chin, yanked her in to hiss words for her ears alone:

"When you told vile lies to my wife, you signed your death warrant." His spittle pelted her neck. "You dirty whore."

Bridget tried to remain strong, show no emotion; but she could not stop the flinch that ran like a flame across her limbs.

The reverend felt it too, and predator that he was, he responded: his dirty teeth grazed her neck, his legs closed like a vice around her skirts. She thought he would lift the fabric, take her right there in front of them all. It would only be proof she was a seductress, the devil's woman.

His tongue touched her flesh, and a furious fire tore its way through Bridget. She wished to be consumed into ash, if only to escape this.

Perhaps her fire burned Harper as well: the reverend jerked away, as if she suddenly repulsed him. Then he clutched her wrists behind her back and pushed her forward. Toward the men, away from her home.

As they stumbled through the trees, Bridget could not keep her eyes closed. She made out faces she wished not to. There he was, holding two torches, one which must have been the reverend's:

Lucas. His gaze met Bridget's for a moment, then turned. He would marry Abigail, Bridget supposed. The mugwort and pennyroyal had not worked.

Reverend Harper brought her to a sudden halt just before the oak marked with a heart in its wood. "Gather kindling," he ordered his congregation. "This whore must not sicken the minds or bodies of any more of our womenfolk." His hands tightened around her wrists, red-hot pincers, as he pronounced:

"The witch burns."

The men tethered Bridget to the tree with thick rope. Fear and her own fire overtook her, so when they touched their torches to the kindling at her feet, she barely registered the added warmth. She barely heard the sound that ripped from the sky, like the cry of a wronged, wrathful woman. She barely felt the sudden downpour soothing her hot flesh, soaking her bones and extinguishing the flames below her.

Hands fumbled at the ropes that held her, a familiar voice whispered in her ear:

"Run."

Bridget ran, but before she did, she touched her hands to the heart-shaped knot in the oak. This tree would not burn, now; it would exist long after Reverend Harper and his entire village were gone.

Bridget was not a witch, but she poured every ounce of power she possessed into that throbbing, beating heart of wood. A part of her soul would remain here, in the woods she loved, forevermore.

***

Three hundred years in the future, Laura's skull rolled over the heart-shaped knot in the oak, and she woke up. The foul-breathed, coarse-sleeved man was gone. It was only Jake Harper, smelling like meat and boy, slipping a hand under her tank top and thrusting his pelvis into hers.

"Jake," she mumbled against his lips pressed to hers, "Jake, wait, I'm not sure—"

"Shh, relax. Doesn't it feel good?" Jake's fingers neared her nipples, his other hand cupped her ass. His sweat stunk of the barbecue she'd run into the woods to avoid. Bile lingered like a half-forgotten memory behind her tongue. The answer flew out of her:

"No."

Laura barely knew Jake. When he touched her, her heart beat with trepidation, not excitement. She didn't want her first time to be out here in the woods, with a guy who was only looking for a warm female body to hold.

"Okay, okay," Jake murmured, moving his lips further down. "Then tell me what would feel good."

Laura couldn't answer, could only think of getting her hands on that heart in the oak. If she could just manage that, she would somehow know what to do. She wrestled her arms free, reached up and behind to where her head still rested against the heart-shaped knot—

The wood pulsed like a real heart, and echoes shot through her. Memories of a flame-eyed woman, standing tall before a world that wished to burn her.

Fire ran across centuries, carrying its heat, its power, from Bridget's veins into hers. Laura let go of the heart to push Jake, harder this time, till he stumbled.

"You actually listening to me," she said with no waver to her voice. "That would feel good."

"Geez." Jake pouted and rubbed his chest as though she'd truly hurt him. He looked, suddenly, like a spoiled little boy. "If I'd known you were such a prude…" The pout turned into a grin. "Or do you play for the other team?"

Fire licked Laura's insides till she didn't care what Jake Harper thought, even if he was more popular than her. "Go fuck yourself, Jake," she said. "Leave me alone."

His eyes narrowed, dark and mean-spirited, and Laura was sure it wasn't a trick of the light this time. "Give me my jacket back, then," he said and started to grab for it, but she was faster, taking it from her shoulders and flinging it toward him.

So much for Jake the courteous gentleman.

He turned and stomped away, pausing after a few steps to spit into the dirt. The loogie glowed grotesquely in the moonlight. "You know, my family practically owns this town," he said. "We have for centuries. You should be grateful I'll even talk to you."

Laura didn't bother to respond, just waited for Jake to vanish. Thank God she hadn't given more than a kiss to someone so pathetic.

Alone in the moonlight, Laura wrapped her arms around the oak tree, rested her head against its rough but tender heart, and let the fire fill her.

Half-Mile- H. Everend

"I'll stall them! Get into those nearby woods!" Sam tore his green eyes from mine. Loud hollering and whoops were headed our way. "GO NOW!"

Snatching the worn handle of my duffle bag, I dashed to the tree line, leaves already brown and dying. Autumn was coming early. In the distance, Sam's F-150 refused to start, the ignition rebuffing his attempts. Revving engines were getting closer. I knew what I had to do at this point: make it to the border between Idaho and Oregon. If I was successful, there would be someone waiting for me to take me to Ashland, which was about a seven-hour drive.

When Sam's truck began making grinding sounds and acting like it was out of gas, he called Julia to change our plans, saying he would try to get us to the state border and everything else would go as planned. Sam and I had a plan for any scenario that could occur. Let's just say

Idaho is not… the most friendly for medical abortion procedures, which is why I'm fleeing to Oregon to get one done.

"There's the truck! Stop them!" Angry, surly voices were nearby. Squealing tires and car doors slamming against rickety metal frames sounded in the night air, approaching Sam's F-150.

I knew I needed to run, but I couldn't help worrying about Sam. We both knew the tremendous risk he was taking by aiding me. He adamantly said he didn't care what others would think of him; he was the only person I knew who would stand by me. Rape was abhorrent to him and because of our state's laws, there was no exception for me to get a medical abortion done.

"It's a blessing deemed by God," one politician said once the trigger law went into effect. "This is something He intended to happen. And we won't allow any unborn child to suffer."

Two bangs broke me from my thoughts, followed by screams of pain. My legs started moving before my brain realized what could have been going on. I was worried about Sam, and what could have happened, but there wasn't any time to waste. All the sacrifice and effort he made would be for naught if I stood around waiting to get caught.

Trying to be silent but quick was more challenging than I realized. I couldn't risk turning my phone's flashlight on yet, and the sky was not helping me with the heavy cloud cover. No moon or stars could peek through. I would have to do the best I could in order to get away undetected.

"She's not here!" someone shouted, but it was faint. I was making better ground than I realized. It was helpful, as the trees in this part of the woods were sparse. My foot hit something hard, causing me to tumble forward and smack into what I only assumed was a tree stump. Something sharp hit the side of my stomach and it sent a ripping sensation through my entire body. Involuntarily, I let out a ragged scream of pain, but quickly covered my mouth. I couldn't afford to be caught.

"Did someone hear that?" My breath came in heavy pants behind my hands. The pain was sharp, like a thousand knives stabbing me at once. I felt a sticky warmth on my stomach and near my abdomen. The rusty stench confirmed what I already knew to be true. This was not good. I would be slowed down for sure.

"She has to be in the woods!" someone yelled.

My whole body locked up, including my thoughts. Realizing my predicament, I had no choice but to turn my light on. I was so close; failure was not an option at this point. There was no way those pro-forced birthers were going to drag me back and force me to birth a rapist's baby! Especially after they told me, I wouldn't even have custody of said child afterward. Hell no! If I was going to be forced to deliver, I would do whatever I could to make sure he or she didn't end up with the man who forced this on me.

Taking a few shaky steps, I pulled my phone from my duffle bag and flipped the flashlight on. *Keep it low to the ground*, I thought. Every step was unbearable. Taking a second, I flashed the light on where it hurt and gagged at the sight: my shirt was torn, blood staining what remained of it, my skin, and the top of my jeans. A significant gouge was visible in the light. This would require many stitches and at least a couple of days in the hospital.

The sound of rushing footsteps on dead leaves caught my full attention before they came to a halt. They were not very far away. "This is warm blood! Unless it's some kind of animal, this has to be her!"

"You don't think she…"

I was too scared to move. They were too close for comfort. I needed to get moving. If I stayed like a deer caught in headlights, that would be the end of my freedom. Mentally, I demanded my feet move forward to get away from the danger nearby.

"Did you hear that?"

Fuck. My brain kicked into fight-or-flight mode, and I took off running faster than a rabbit being chased by a wolf. Crunching leaves and my heavy breathing drowned out everything else around me. My lungs were burning, and my side was signaling my brain about its searing pain; it gave me the sensation as though I was on fire.

"I think that's her! Let's go! She killed a baby!"

Get to the border! I screamed mentally. *Get to the border! Julia will help you! You can't let Sam down!* My legs felt like jello; my lungs were blazing. Grass and tree branches turned to pavement, and I realized I was on Yturri Boulevard. Slowing my steps for a second, I flashed my phone's pathetic flashlight in the surrounding area. Something caught in its dim lighting: a huge green and white sign stood about 25 yards in front of me. "Welcome to Oregon" it read.

I did it. I fucking did it! Now there was nothing those redneck bastards could do to me now. Speaking of the crowd chasing me, either I got farther ahead than I thought or they gave up on me. It was eerily silent.

Didn't Sam say Julia would meet us at the border? I'm guessing they meant near this sign here? Or maybe it's somewhere else. Glancing around the area, it was dark and empty except for my light. *I could try to call her, but the cell service—*

A pair of bright lights flicked on from behind the sign. My heart sank in my stomach. There was nowhere for me to go.

"Blair?" a female voice rang out. "Sam's friend?"

Panicked relief replaced fear as I stumbled toward the woman. She had flowing auburn hair that reminded me of cotton. There was plenty of gray peeking through, but it gave her a sophisticated look. Julia appeared to be in her upper 40s to early 50s. She was an angel sent to me.

"I got you!" Julia whispered as I fell into her arms. My breathing was irregular, along with my muscles aching. All I wanted to do in that moment was close my eyes and go to sleep. Then I remembered the mob after me. Pulling myself away from her, I made my way to the passenger door, panic clear in my eyes.

"We have to go! They're after me! They'll take me back to Boise and force me to stay in a hospital until I deliver this child! I can't do that." I inhaled sharply before continuing. "Believe me, I don't condone this. But I also didn't condone to be raped against my will and force to carry my rapist's baby only for him to gain custody once everything was said and done–"

"It's okay, Blair." She cut me off, a ghost of a smile on her face. "You don't need to explain your circumstances to me. Everyone has their own reasons." Julia put the car into gear and started speeding toward Jordan Valley. "First things first. We need to get you medical attention. Don't worry. I know just the place that will take care of everything. And then we'll make our way to Ashland.

I couldn't help but ask, "Am I safe? Will they remove this baby from me?"

"It's not a baby yet, and yes, they will get it safely removed, and you can go back to your life as it was before all this."

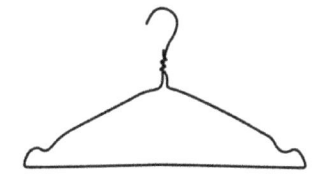

The Heartbeat- Melinda N. Brunson

It was a typical Tuesday morning in the Young household. Danny was in the kitchen making a quick breakfast, while Melody helped their daughter get ready for pre-school. "Pancakes are ready!" echoed up the stairs as mother and daughter made their way down.

"Thank you, Daddy," Claire's sweet little three-year-old voice sang, as she sat down at the table. The couple sat down across from their daughter, smiles on their lips as they held hands.

"Just think, there will be two of them before we know it," Danny said dreamily as he pulled his wife's hand to his lips. She smiled and let a peaceful sigh out. They had been trying for two and a half years, ever since their daughter's first birthday. After four failed rounds of non-invasive fertility treatment, they finally had a positive test. Forty-six positive tests to be exact, including the three that she had taken the previous morning. There had been so many negative ones, that Melody had a difficult time believing the positive tests and even the blood work she had around six weeks.

"I know," she said softly, "and I cannot wait to finally see our little bean for the first time today." She exhaled, turning back to the breakfast in front of her.

As they finished their pancakes, Melody could not help but let the negative thoughts fill her mind. Her first pregnancy was so easy and felt like a dream. They waited so long and were rewarded with a healthy pregnancy and beautiful little girl. This pregnancy felt different. She'd been nauseous the entire second run with the fertility medication. The fifth round being the hardest, but the one that ended with a positive test. She'd felt ill every day – nauseous, tired, and mentally not quite herself. She was so grateful for having this life inside of her, but secretly she was also terrified. So much had changed in the world since her pregnancy with Claire.

If something had gone wrong four years ago, Melody would have had choices. She would have had rights over her own body. In the days leading up to this positive test, though, the laws across the country changed, especially in the state where she lived. If anything went wrong, after six weeks, there would be nothing that she could do. She could even be accused of causing harm and be punished by law. These were the thoughts running through her mind. Every day. She tried to stay positive for her husband and daughter. This was an exciting time for them. The odds of anything happening were so low, but she just could not let the thoughts of *what if* leave her mind.

      The family loaded into their car and headed towards pre-school. They dropped Claire off, sending her inside with hugs, kisses, and promises of bringing pictures of the baby when they pick her up. The doctors' office was not too far from the school, and the couple's favorite coffee shop was on the way. They stopped for their morning coffees, taking their time getting to the parking deck beside the office.

      "Are you ready?" Danny opened his wife's door, putting his hand out for her.

      With a little reluctance, she took it. "I'm nervous," she said, standing beside him. "What if…" she started, only to be stopped by a sudden kiss upon her lips. She sighed, giving in to the reassuring affection. Their lips parted, and their eyes met.

      "Everything is going to be fine," he said in a calm, confident voice. "You are an amazing mother, a good person. We are good people and have done everything right." He caressed her cheek, and pulled her close, wrapping his arms around her shoulders. "Everything is going to be fine."

The woman took a deep breath, nodding at his words and trying to push the negative thoughts away. "Okay. Let's go." She pulled back, and their hands intertwined as they began walking towards the door.

It was always a little awkward getting started for a prenatal appointment. Peeing in a cup, being weighed, having blood drawn… Awkward, but important. Every time. After the work up routine, the nurse took the couple into the ultrasound room. Melody laid on the table, her bottom half covered with a sheet, and Danny sat at her side holding her hand. They sat in silence for a few moments, anxious, silently speaking positivity into the universe. Then the doctor came in.

"Mr. and Mrs. Young, it is so good to see you here again!" She was kind and warm, Dr. Cohen, and had been with them through their ten-year fertility journey. When Melody felt broken and like a failure, she was there to remind her she was not and how strong she was for going through so much to bring a new life into the world. "It looks like we had great bloodwork at our estimated six weeks," the doctor said as she looked over the charts, "and now that we should be at twelve weeks, it is time to take look. Are we ready?" The couple nodded, both taking and hold a deep breath as the image began to appear on the screen. The doctor looked around, noting that fluid looked good, the placenta looked great. She pointed out tiny hands, tiny feet, a cute little nose. "Okay, let's get that little heartbeat!"

She moved the wand around, zooming in on her screen. Her brows furrowed a little, she clicked. There was no sound. She adjusted the wand again. Clicked. No sound. She tried again. No. Sound. "I... um..." her eyes looked to glass over, filling with tears as she looked back to the couple. "I am so sorry. There's no heartbeat."

Melody's grip tightened around husband's hand as they saw what looked like a beautiful, healthy baby appear on the sonogram screen. She'd let her breath go, and her anxiety was beginning to turn to excitement. Then as the doctor's face began to change, she felt a cold chill run down her spine. *"There's no heartbeat."* The words hit her like a stack of cinderblocks and echoed through her ears like a fire alarm. Her face went flush, and tears began to stream down her face.

"No, no that's not possible," her husband said, now standing, holding her hand with both of his. "Please... Check again." The doctor checked again and looked back to him shaking her head. "No. No! We did everything… we did everything right..." his voice trailed off as he sat back down in disbelief.

Melody looked over to him, and then back to the doctor. "I don't understand. I had three positive tests yesterday morning. There have been no signs of a… a loss. I…" The woman's words were shaky as the little bit of hope that she had went away. "I have done everything that I should. Dr. Cohen… I have a daughter at home. What, what do we do? I didn't do anything wrong…" She searched the doctor's face for answers, for anything, but she looked back at them in disbelief.

"I don't know," the woman's voice broke as she continued, "This is the first time since everything changed. Melody, I don't know…"

Melody cleaned herself up, putting her pants back on, as all three adults stayed in the room in shock. She began to pace about, realizing that her worst nightmares were about to come true. "What if we lie?" Melody looked towards the doctor. "You could just say there was a heartbeat, and then we can have time to figure it out… We can move… We can do something."

Dr. Cohen wiped the tears from her own face. "I'm afraid I can't. The computers automatically upload as we do the scan. I cannot do anything." She picked up the one picture that printed, noticing a blinking on the monitor, and handed it to her patient. "I am so sorry… You do not deserve any of this." She looked back at the monitor and then to the couple. "You must leave. Now. An alert has been sent through the system. I do not know how much time you have."

She grabbed Danny's arm, pulling him up from his despair and pushing him towards the door. "Hurry. Go through the fire exit. Go get Claire. Go!" The doctor opened the door, checking for a clear path and sent the Youngs down the hallway. She then closed the door and went across the hallway to her office, sat down with the chart for a minute, and then picked up the phone just as security showed up at her door. "I was just about to call… They are in room 2 across the hall," she said in a calm voice, despite her heart beating in her throat. She could only hope that the couple made it out without being seen, as she convinced the officers that they were just there, before they began calling for back up on their radios. In their car and headed down the road already, the couple had never been more grateful for a ground level doctor's office. Their hearts were aching, and minds racing. If this had been thirteen weeks ago, they would be driving home to get an overnight bag and arrange care for Claire. They would be returning to the hospital in a few hours, to have a procedure, say goodbye, and go home in the morning. Now though, they felt like they were running for their lives. "Did you call the school already?" Danny asked, as they turned into the pre-school driveway.

"Yes," Melody replied, "I called as soon as we left the building. They will be at the door with her." As they pulled up, Claire and her teacher were standing at the curb waiting. "Thank you, so much, family emergencies happen so suddenly," she said as Claire was buckled into her seat. As they began pulling out of the school, the sky started to darken, and a rumble shook their car.

"Mommy…" the little voice from the back seat called, "What's that?" Melody looked back at her daughter and then out of the window where she was pointing. A mass of dark clouds was roiling just down the street, lighting struck, and a set of red eyes appeared. "Oh my God, Danny! DRIVE!" she exclaimed to her husband, as the child began to cry. She unbuckled her seat belt and went into the backseat to comfort her daughter. "Love, it's okay. Don't worry… Mommy is here." She wiped the little girls tears away, kissing her forehead and cheeks. "I won't let anything happen to you. Okay?" As they continued down the road, Melody held onto her daughter's hand, kissing her head and promising to keep her safe. Speeding onto the interstate, the darkness steadily crept closer to them, regardless of how fast they drove. It didn't seem to affect any of the other vehicles on the road, in fact the people passing the opposite direction didn't seem to notice anything was wrong.

"How do they not see this?!" The man was flabbergasted. They were literally being chased by what can only be described as a monster, and nobody seemed to notice or care.

"Because it's only after us… After me… I am so sorry." She reached forward, placing her hand on his shoulder. "I don't know what I did wrong… But it must be my fault."

He shook his head. "No. You didn't do anything wrong. This kind of thing doesn't happen to good people… It doesn't. We'll go somewhere safe…" She squeezed his shoulder, holding back the tears that ached to flow. She had to be strong, she had to hold it together for her daughter. The nauseousness she'd been fighting for weeks began to settle in. Melody took a few deep breaths and leaned back against the seat. Still holding Claire's hand, she closed her eyes for a few minutes.

"Mommy?" the sweet little voice asked. "Yes, sweetheart?" she said groggily. "Why did you kill our baby?"

Melody's eyes shot open as her daughter's sweet voice deepened and became metallic and broken. "What?!" She immediately sat up and turned to the car seat. The beautiful blue eyes of her baby had turned crimson as her alabaster skin disappeared into darkness. "CLAIRE! DANNY, HELP!" She tried to pull her hand away, but a black claw held tight. "DANNY!" She reached for his shoulder, only to pull darkness towards her. She peered into the front of the car, it was stopped in a parking lot and her husband was nowhere to be found. "No… Let me go!" The woman kicked and pulled to get out of the grasp of this monster that was filling her backseat.

As the darkness surrounded her more and more, she felt it grasp her arms. She couldn't move. "Please…" she cried, tears streaming uncontrollably down her face, "I did everything right… I want this baby… I want this family. My daughter and husband need me… Please…"

The crimson eyes peered into hers, fangs showing and dripping black goo. It hissed, "You don't deserve this baby… You wished it away… You killed it!"

"NO! Never… I was just so scared of what if…" she cried.

"You are WEAK!" the darkness hissed. "You deceived your husband! You failed your daughter! You are NOT worthy of ANY of them, and now you will never see them again!"

Melody's tears of sadness and pleading became tears of anger. She'd given everything to conceive this child, to have the opportunity to grow it in her womb and give it life, to give her daughter a sibling and herself and husband a second child. She nurtured and nourished her body to take care of this baby, despite her fears. She did nothing wrong… "I'VE DONE NOTHING WRONG!" she screamed at the top of her lungs, only to not be heard. As she opened her mouth the darkness began filling her lungs, and the claws grasped her tighter and tighter, digging into her skin, until her consciousness went away. It had consumed her entire existence.

One week later, Melody's groggy eyes slowly opened. The room was abnormally bright, and white. She blinked several times and tried to reach for her face to rub her eyes. Her hands would not move. As she became more and more conscious, a familiar voice filled her ears. "My love, shh... it's okay, you're okay." Danny appeared at her side. He moved a few pieces of loose hair from her face and smiled a gentle smile. "Love, you passed out and started losing blood in the car… I had to take you to the hospital."

She looked at him, feeling both comforted by his presence and confused about what was going on. She tried to get a few words out, but her throat was so dry. He picked up a cup and straw, allowing her to sip some water. With her throat not as scratchy she spoke, "There was a monster, I was… dead… I'm sure of it… What's happening?" She tried to lift her hands again, and then was able to see the restraints on her wrists. "They had to sedate and detain you for several days, until the bleeding stopped, and test results came back from our appointment last week. Melody, the baby had a genetic anomaly and must have passed while we slept the night before our scan. Everything is going to be okay. Now that you are awake, we can go back home today. Your parents are there with Claire."

A nurse came in and released the restraints as Danny spoke to his wife. Immediately after the nurse left, the couple embraced, sobbing and grieving together in the way that they should have been able to a week ago. "I'm so sorry that this happened, that these laws are happening… Nobody deserves this," he said, an edge of anger in his sincerity. "We will fight to make this right. For you. For our daughter. Whatever it takes." She held him tighter, realizing how differently the situation could have turned out.

The darkness was going to take her away, for something that she had no control over. Just like it took the control away from women and their right to choices. She squeezed her eyes closed and opened them again, hoping that maybe this was all a horrible nightmare, only to find herself still in her husband's arms on a hospital bed. "I'm ready to go home," she said, leaning back and wiping the tears from her cheeks, "and to do whatever we can to make sure that Claire or any other woman never has to go through this." He nodded in agreement and pulled her into his arms again. "Whatever it takes."

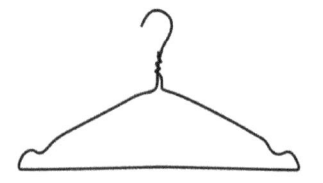

The Burden- Angel Krause

    I don't remember when I lost feeling in my fingers. It may have been the first two full minutes I sat clenching the blanket over my head. Just as likely, it could have been any of the moments that followed. That horrible squelching sound. As time moved forward, I sat frozen in my bed. All I could feel instead of my breaths, were my knees pressed tightly against my chest. I don't think I could have opened my eyes if I wanted to.

    All I can hear is the sound. Like boots thick with mud, there was a 'splat' after 'splat' against the cheap linoleum floor of my apartment. In any situation like this, someone might have investigated. There might have been a phone call or a yell. Something, I'm certain, meant to scare off the noise or prove it was actually nothing at all.

    Not this time. No, I know this sound well. The hollow moaning that we react to as a human sound, all the while knowing it is anything but. It wasn't a human. It wasn't alive. I can hear the mass of gunk hit the door of my bedroom and I jump. I even yelp in surprise. Tears are streaming down my face and all I can think is, *why now?*

I remember the first time I ever heard noises like this. I remember the first time I sat in a bed just like this and was scared to open my eyes. It was an eerie sense of haunting. A distant memory of something I couldn't let go of. A girl left abandoned. A woman left judged. The first time I heard this sound was thirteen years ago.

***

"When you get here, you'll have to go to the back parking lot. Someone will come out to escort you inside."

Silence. That was all the woman on the phone heard next. Was this really happening? Was I really doing this? As the phone call ended, the phone dropped from my hand. Silence surrounded me as I rested my head on my steering wheel and screamed out in fear. I never knew such sadness. Even in the years that followed.

My eyes were bloodshot by the time I stopped crying. The sound returned as I tried to find the phone I had dropped before. I remember the next call. I can still hear the sound of his voice when he answers.

"I thought you'd call to tell me that," he says, cold and overly confident.

"What?" The voice I use is not my own. It was something I've seen described in stories my entire life. Only now was it something I really understood.

"I knew there was a chance…" he says, attempting to sound more concerned than his original response.

"Di-did you do this on purpose?" The confusion is clear, and the shards of my broken heart have risen like bile in my throat. Scratching and tearing into my insides.

"I thought I was going to lose you." That was really the last thing I heard.

The rest of it didn't matter. In a desperate attempt to keep me, my idiotic nineteen-year-old boyfriend had lied. He hadn't pulled out in time. He had intentionally planted a seed that he expected me to suck up and nurture. No. Not me. Not at this age. Not at this point in my life.

What life would a child even have with me? What would the future hold? I lost my composure once more. I was certain, at any given moment, I was going to lose the ability to sob altogether. The tears would run dry and maybe I'd become numb if only to get a break from this crippling slew of emotions.

I told no one but my best friend. I dealt with it entirely alone otherwise. I did as they said. I went to the back door. There were people outside with signs. My goddess, the things they said. Murderers. Anyone who came to this place was a murderer. I'm only grateful the inside staff was so kind. They were so patient and judgment free. In the world of darkness around me, their small tokens of compassion gave me hope. Maybe I wasn't all the things everyone said.

My parents were certainly against this sort of thing. I even had a sister that couldn't get pregnant. What would she think if she knew? I picked and picked and picked at my fingers, scratching at my cuticles until they began to shimmer with blood. I looked around and saw the faces of those around me. Those who were there for any number of reasons.

I saw the fourteen-year-old girl there in shambles with her parents. I saw plenty of others just there for birth control or checkups. Not everyone was there to do this. And yet? I also realized I wasn't alone. It gave me a false sense of comfort. I was early. I was able to do it the easier of the two methods and all I had to do was take a pill. Something I was completely disconnected from. Well, at least until the pain started.

"It'll be just like a period but heavier and maybe a little more painful."

That is what they had told me. And even with the pamphlets, the short therapy session, and all the information in the world, I was completely unprepared. The cramping started after the blood. I remember the spotting quite vividly and I remember that was the first sting of guilt. No more. The fucked-up situation I had found myself in was no longer going to be at the forefront of my problems. Or was it?

I didn't feel relieved. I wasn't grateful for the loss. I felt guilt. I felt shame. I felt sad. I always knew I wanted to be a mother and now I was willingly flushing that down the toilet. Literally. What if this meant no children later? What if this ruined my life? What if something goes wrong and it ends up surviving? What about birth defects? What about endangering my own life? What if my parents find out?

Those were all the things I asked myself as I rolled over in pain in my bed. Heating pad pressed tight against my abdomen, I flipped channels to find a distraction. Nothing worked. The pain I felt physically was nothing to the beating I was giving myself mentally. I went to church when I was younger. I had always believed what I had done was a sin. A horrible one. I couldn't have known what would happen back then. I certainly didn't understand all the other medical pieces that went into women's health that weren't as simple as giving up a baby. I was so stupid. Maybe the universe thought I needed a lesson.

It was that night the squelch came from downstairs. In those days I had a roommate and we lived in a townhouse. She was out of town, thankfully. Well, I was thankful at first. At the sounds shifted, I became scared. I was alone and more than a little vulnerable. The pain intensified as I heard what I can only recall being the sounds of wet towels slapping the wall. It was sludging its way up the stairs and I tried to lean forward to find my phone.

Naturally I yanked the heating pad with me, and it tangled with the lamp, knocking it to the floor. The flickering light focused around the edge of my bed and I could see just past it to the doorway. The moaning started then. My eyes wide, as my entire body fell backwards into the pillows at what I was seeing. There was only a short break from the pain I felt.

In front of the door, not five feet from my bed, was a giant puddle of red. At first, it appeared to be just blood. As my eyes adjusted to the flickering light, I soon realized it wasn't that simple. The mass was concocted of tissue and other various colors of matter. It started small, but as it squelched towards me, it grew in mass. The first pink arm that reached out to the end of my bed was when I finally yanked the covers over my face.

Funny, isn't it? Even in the adult world, we live in childhood fantasies of comfort and safety. No such grace for me. I had done an awful thing and my guilt was going to show me exactly how much pain I deserved.

This mass of regret showed itself every night for six months. Each time, getting just a little closer to me. It was agonizing. I remember that. I remember hating when dark came, and I remember the insomnia that followed the fear. I couldn't tell anyone. Who the fuck would believe me? Yet every night it came. Suctioning to the stairs and calling out to me. Reminding me of what I had done.

It was well over a year before I found any peace. I knew by then I had made the right choice. I knew it was the right thing to do. It also led me to a much safer path with partners. I didn't trust anyone after that. Lessons learned; I suppose.

***

So, the question is, why is it back? This time, I didn't feel the silence following the sounds. I didn't notice a shift in the air. Instead, I was forced to tighten my grip on the bedding as it was yanked from the bed. I grunted out in response, but it was clear I was no match. I had been under the covers for so long, I almost forgot the lights were on. My lids were illuminated. I trusted it. I trusted the light as some sense of beacon of security. As my eyes opened, I glanced at where the blanket had been pulled from my form.

Tears flooded my eyes. My heart was racing so hard, I could barely feel it. My mouth opened but I couldn't form noises. Feeling my hands fall to the bed besides me, they knotted up against the mattress. My legs were eager to push further into my chest, but there was simply no room. The guilt had returned. She sat upon my bed, a disaster of a memory. The blob of blood and goo was now moving steadily towards me. This time she grew arms, her messy tissue scratching at the bed to get closer to me.

This time, the center wasn't just a mash up of colors and textures. This time, she had a misshapen head. There were parts that were round, but most of it was empty and black. Parts of the mass, which was now so large it covered half of my bed, had clumps of hair and even teeth. None of this made sense. This couldn't possibly be real. I had barely thought about the past.

This is the part of the situation where people yell at the screen to run.

'Get out of there.'
'Why isn't she moving?'

I couldn't move. I wasn't in control anymore. In this moment, the guilt and fear had completely taken over. The decrepit hand slid up my thigh and connected to my belly. The pain I felt in that moment was sharp and unexpected. I called out in anguish. My hands grabbed the mess of a wrist I found there. Was this how it was supposed to be?

"Stop!" I called out, louder and stronger than I had thought I was capable of.

I must have yelled stop thirty times. A noise in the distance called me out of my pain. The sweet sound of birds and piano music filled my ears and my eyes opened in a groggy state. "Motherfucker," I groan.

The alarm I had set for work is warning me that I now have less time to get ready than usual. I sat up in bed and touched my face. My legs. I touched my stomach. Nothing was there. No proof of the thing I had experienced in the night. I didn't know relief. Just a girl left abandoned. A woman left judged.

Today is the day after Roe V Wade has been overturned. All of these people with their opinions on my body and now all of my guilt has resurfaced. All the pain and fear I had back then has now returned tenfold. Was this the new world? Women robbed of control over their own bodies? Forced to feel anger and fear and torment over decisions they make in order for a better life? Even though it has been twelve years since I have known that fear and that guilt, it has returned stronger than before.

    I don't regret my decision. I made a choice. A very difficult choice. It was mine to make. I fear for the women whose health will be put in jeopardy over this. The women and young girls who will be mistreated and abused for such mistakes. The guilt I carry is no longer my own. It has transformed into a burden I carry for the women in my country. Their fear and pain are now my own.

    As I wipe tears from my eyes, my final alarm goes off. I feel as though I am in mourning. My body feels as though I was in a car accident. The floor is chilly to my bare feet but that isn't what catches me off guard. My hand slides down the side of my bed. My fingertips brush against something thick and cold. A dark red and milky substance coats my bedding and trails from the corner all the way to the door. This new burden was making a statement. She was telling me she is here to stay. So long as women are left without a voice, she will remain my constant torment.

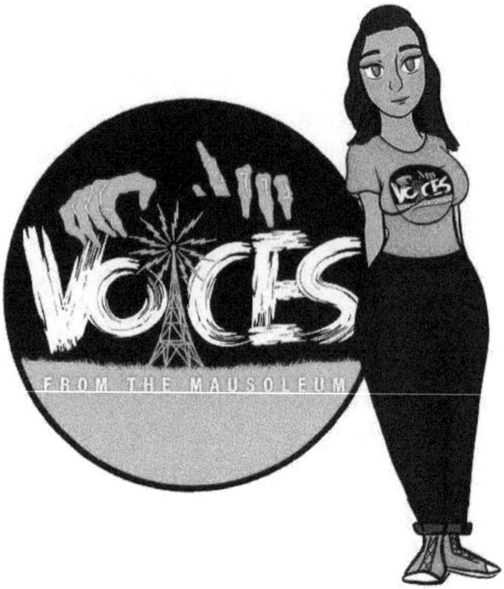
VOICES
FROM THE MAUSOLEUM

Lightning Source UK Ltd.
Milton Keynes UK
UKHW011430181222
414118UK00001B/14